'Berlie Doherty has magic in l
Junior Bookshelf

Berlie Doherty is a distinguished writer for young people and twice winner of the prestigious Carnegie Medal for *Granny was a Buffer Girl* and *Dear Nobody*. A former teacher, Berlie Doherty has also worked in schools broadcasting and adult education. She has also written several books for adults and numerous plays for radio, theatre and television.

Praise for *Street Child*, the companion novel to *Far From Home*:
'A terrific adventure story, heart-warmingly poignant and a tribute to the resilience of the human spirit. A magnificent story.'
Daily Mail

FAR FROM HOME

The Sisters *of* STREET CHILD

BERLIE DOHERTY

HarperCollins *Children's Books*

First published in Great Britain by HarperCollins *Children's Books* 2015
HarperCollins *Children's Books* is a division of HarperCollins*Publishers* Ltd,
HarperCollins Publishers
1 London Bridge Street
London SE1 9GF
The HarperCollins *Children's Books* website address is
www.harpercollins.co.uk

2

Far From Home
Text copyright © Berlie Doherty 2014

The author asserts the moral right to be identified as the author of this work.

ISBN-13 978-0-00-757882-5

Printed and bound in England by
Clays Ltd, St Ives plc

MIX
Paper from
responsible sources
FSC® C007454

CONTENTS

For Tommy, Hannah, Kasia,
Anna-Merryn, Eda, Leo and Tess

I would like to thank all the hundreds of children
who have written to me over the years since
Street Child was first published, asking what
happened to Emily and Lizzie. I hope this
answers your question!

I would also like to thank HarperCollins
for commissioning this companion book, and in
particular my editors Lizzie Clifford and
Lauren Buckland for their enthusiasm and
encouragement while I was writing it.

Tell Me Your Story, Emily and Lizzie

We're Emily and Lizzie Jarvis. We're sitting by the window in our room. Outside, we can hear a soft kind of sighing, like the wind in the trees, though we know it isn't that really. It's a comforting sound, and it's lulling us to sleep. But we can't sleep yet. There's so much to think about first, so much to talk about. So much remembering to do.

Would you like to know our story?

There used to be five of us in our family, and now there's only two. After Pa died we had to move into a room in a big, crowded tenement house with Ma and our little brother, Jim, and we just managed to keep going because Ma got a job as cook in a Big House. But then she fell ill and she had to stop working. There was no money left to live on, no money for the rent. She gave her last coin to Jim and told him to buy a nice pie for us all, full of meat and gravy.

9

He was so excited. He was too young to understand that Ma thought it was the last good meal we would ever have. But she couldn't eat it, she was too ill.

And then the owner of the room came for the rent, and when he saw Ma's empty purse, and her too sick to earn anything, he turned us out on the streets. Where was there to go? Ma took us to the Big House, down the steps to the kitchen, and she begged her friend Rosie to look after us. And then she told us we must stay there, without her. She must take Jim with her, and she must leave us behind. It broke her heart to tell us that, we knew. It breaks our hearts to think about it. But we must think about it. We must tell our story, every bit of it, so we never forget what it was like for us before we came here.

This is our story.

1

TAKE US WITH YOU, MA

"Take us with you, Ma! Don't leave us here!" Lizzie begged.

"I can't," her mother said. She didn't turn round. "Bless you, I can't. This is best for you. God bless you, both of you."

Mrs Jarvis took Jim's hand and bundled him quickly out of the door. It swung shut behind them with a loud thud.

Immediately Lizzie broke into howls of grief. "Ma! Ma! Don't leave us behind!" she sobbed. "Don't go without us!"

She tried to wrench open the door, but her sister put her arms round her, holding her tight. "It's all right. It's all right, Lizzie," she whispered.

"We might never see them again!" Lizzie shook her away and covered her face with her hands. She didn't want to see anything, didn't want to hear anything.

"I know. It's just as bad for me," Emily said. "I didn't want her to go. I didn't want Jim to go." Her voice was breaking up now; tiny rags of sound like brave little flags in the wind. "But Ma had no choice, did she? She wants to save us; that's what she said. She brought us here so Rosie can take care of us."

Rosie, their mother's only friend in the world, came over to the two girls and drew them away from the door. "I'll do my best," she told them. She sat them down at the kitchen table where she had been making bread for the master of the house. She started smoothing flour away with the wedge of her hand, then tracing circles into it with her plump fingers. It was as if she was looking for words there to help her. All that could be heard were the shivering sobs that Lizzie made.

"Listen, girls," Rosie said at last. "Your ma's ill. You know that, don't you? She ain't going to get better."

Lizzie stifled another sob. This time she let Emily creep her hand into her own, and squeezed and squeezed to keep the unimaginable pain of those words away.

"And you heard what Judd said? She's the housekeeper, and what she says, goes. She's the law round here, she is. She said she'd let you stay a bit, if you keep quiet and hidden, but not for ever. She can't be feeding two grown girls on his lordship's money, now, can she? She'd lose her job if he found out you were here, and so would I. I'll do what I can for you, I promise, but I really don't know what it is I *can* do. But at the very least I'll save you from the streets, or even worse than that, from a life in the workhouse." She shuddered, rubbing her stout upper arms vigorously as if the thought of the workhouse had chilled her bones. "Never, never. I'll never let you go there, girls."

She flapped her hands along her sleeves to try to dust away the flour.

"Busy, let's be busy! Em'ly, you've got bread to make. See if it's as good as your ma used to make. Lizzie, you've got a floor to sweep because I can't touch flour without getting it everywhere I turn! And I've got a fire to mend. For pity's sake, look at it! It's crawling away like a rat down a hole."

She lifted a pair of bellows from the side of the range and knelt in the hearth, working them into the dying embers to coax the flames back, then threw some knuckles of wood onto the glowing ashes. She sat back, watching the dance of the flames, and listened to the girls behind her. She could hear Emily standing up at last from the bench and starting to knead the dough on the table, popping the air out of it with a sure, firm touch, and at last settling into a rhythm, breathing with a slow kind of satisfaction as she did so. Rosie smiled to herself. *She sounds just like her ma*, she thought. *And nothing ever calmed Annie Jarvis down as much as making bread. I'd enjoy working with Em'ly in the kitchen, if only Judd could find a way of letting her stay. Annie's daughter, working alongside of me. What a pleasure that would be.*

She lifted coals onto the fire, one by one, taking time over her task, not wanting to disturb the girls. At last, she heard Lizzie push the bench away and stand up; heard her gently sweeping the floor with the kitchen broom, scattering drops of water as she went so the dust didn't fly. Rosie turned and saw that tears were still streaming down Lizzie's face, burning her cheeks. "Ma, Ma," she whispered as she worked. "I want you, Ma."

As soon she had finished that task Rosie asked her to help with setting a tray to take upstairs, and with sorting out clean knives, forks and spoons to be locked away by Judd in the silver cabinet. The cutlery jittered in Lizzie's hands, she was so scared of making a mistake, but at last the job was done and Rosie smiled her satisfaction.

"We get along very well in this job, don't we, girls?" she said. "I think I can even sit down for a minute now." She eased herself onto the bench, slipping her boots off, wriggling her toes.

There was the sudden pounding of feet down the stairs, the kitchen door was flung open, and there stood the housekeeper, lips pursed, grey eyes sharp and cold as points of ice. Rosie jumped to her feet, as though she'd sat on a cat.

"His lordship has come in early from his afternoon walk," Judd announced. She jangled the keys that were hanging in a bunch from her belt. "I want you to get these girls out of my sight."

"But he never comes down here, Judd," Rosie said. "And the mistresses are away."

"I said, out of my sight." Judd took in the blazing fire, the clean floor, the dough rising plump as a chicken in the bread tins, and sniffed. "Now! I've never seen them in my life." She turned her back, arms akimbo, so her elbows stuck out sharp and angled in her tight black sleeves.

Rosie took the girls by the hand and hustled them into the pantry. "He *never* comes down to the kitchen," she muttered. "Judd's behaving like a mother goose watching out for the fox. I'll let you out when I can."

She closed the pantry door quietly. The glow of the fire disappeared, and the sisters stood in complete darkness. Lizzie moved, and something thumped against her face. She stifled a shriek of shock, and nervously lifted up her hand to feel what it was, her other hand grasping Emily's arm.

"Ducks!" she whispered, feeling a brace of the birds hanging above their heads. "Dead ducks!" and for some reason all the emotions of the day, the need to be quiet, the strangeness of everything, the knowledge that Emily was standing next to her breathing the same ducky air, and that Judd was watching out for his lordship, the fox; everything about the day welled up in her, until a pent-up explosion of sound burst out of her mouth.

"Are you crying?" Emily whispered.

"No," Lizzie whispered back. Her voice was shaking. Her whole body was shaking. Tears of pain and laughter burnt her cheeks. "I am a bit. But I can't stop giggling, Emily. Can't stop."

2

SAFE TILL MORNING

It seemed as if hours were passing while Emily and Lizzie stood in the dark pantry, listening to the to and fro of bustle in the kitchen: food being scraped off plates, pans being washed, the fire being raked. All this time they daren't move, except to lower themselves away from the dangling ducks and squat down on the cold stone floor. Eventually the door opened a crack, the glow of a candle warmed the darkness, and Rosie's face appeared.

"Me and Judd have finished down here," she whispered. "I'll put some cold meat out for you, and you must eat it before the mice do. There's a water closet in the back yard for your necessaries, and a couple of rugs by the fire, so you can curl up there. Out you come."

She helped them to stand and they stumbled out, stiff and cold, into the cosy firelight of the kitchen. Rosie rubbed their numb hands to warm them up.

Her face was creased with concern. "His lordship's eaten his supper, and he's dozing in front of the fire like he always does when the ladies are away. He'll totter off to bed any time now, so you're quite safe till morning."

"Is his lordship really a lord?" Lizzie asked.

"Heavens, no!" Rosie laughed. "We'd be in a much bigger house if he was, and there'd be servants all over the place. No, he's a barrister or something like, and he can be as grumpy as I don't know what if we get things wrong by mistake." She led the girls over to the table and pushed the plates of meat and potatoes in front of them.

"He makes us feel like criminals sometimes because his coffee's not hot enough or there's too much salt in his potatoes. He hates it when the mistresses are away and there's just him and the two Dearies. He can snap at you like a bear with a sore head sometimes." She sat on the bench next to Lizzie and untied her house boots, letting her toes wriggle deliciously in the air. "Ooh, that's better. Judd's right, he'd put us out on the street, all of us, if he thought we was doing something behind his back, feeding waifs and strays."

"We're not waifs and strays!" Lizzie protested.

"We are now," Emily reminded her. "Where's home, now Mr Spink has kicked us out?"

Rosie undid the ties of her cap and loosened her long, dark hair. She patted Emily's hand and stood up. "*But* he ate every bit of that bread you made, Em'ly, and then asked for more! That's the first time since Annie left off working here. So we've high hopes for you. But then you might do me out of a job, and where would I be? You teach me, just like your ma taught you. It'll take a bit of doing, so I'll need you here a while!" She bent down to pick up her boots, and quickly kissed the tops of their heads. "Good night, girls. God bless."

"I'm too tired to eat anything," Lizzie said when Rosie had gone, locking the door behind her. "I just want to go to sleep, Emily."

"You heard what Rosie said. Eat, before the mice get it. And suppose we get chucked out in the middle of the night? We'll wish we had food in our bellies then, won't we?"

Lizzie swallowed her cold meat dutifully, and Emily did the same. It was good meat, she could tell that, tender and tasty, but every mouthful seemed to clog up her throat and choke her. She cleared the plates away and then curled up next to Lizzie in front of the fire.

"You won't stay here without me, Emily?" Lizzie murmured.

"Course I won't. I'll never leave you, Lizzie." She stared into the pale flicker of the dying flames. "I wonder where Ma and Jim are now?" But Lizzie was already asleep. Images of Ma's face swooned in and out of the darkness. It was as if, for a moment, she was still there with them, until the room grew into its night-time dark around her. "Please, God, let them both be safe," Emily whispered. "Please let someone as kind as Rosie take care of them."

A grey and drizzly dawn was seeping down through the basement window when Rosie shook the girls awake.

"I shall have to move you so's I can get this fire lit," she said. "Let's hope that other nice loaf of yours was cooked proper before it went out, cos I forgot all about it in the excitement. That's my trouble."

"It's all right, Rosie. I saw to it." Emily yawned and opened the oven door to lift out the new loaf, freshly baked and barely cool. It smelled wonderful.

"Just how he likes it!" Rosie marvelled. "He'll be a happy man this morning. He won't be complaining that he's breaking a tooth with every bite of my bread."

Lizzie sat up and huddled the rug round her shoulders. She stared blankly round the strange kitchen, dazed by memories of yesterday: her mother, bent with pain and weakness; her brother, white-faced with shock and sorrow as he was bundled outside; the slam of the door; the sound of her own fists pummelling. *Don't leave us behind! Don't go without us!* Dimly she heard Rosie chattering away as if today was a day like any other.

"There's a pump in the back yard to wash the sleep out of your faces," she was saying. "And while you're out there, you can pump up some water for me to boil for his breakfast tea, Em'ly. Lizzie, here's a bowl of scraps; you can chuck these at the hens in the yard. I've got to fetch coal and get this fire going again. Then we can start the day proper."

It was cold and damp in the yard, with a few sparks of snow in the air. Emily pumped up water to splash on her face, then nodded to Lizzie. Lizzie dipped her face down and then lifted up her head from the water; gasping with cold, her hair damp and clinging to her cheeks.

"Now you'll feel a bit brighter," Emily said. "And you like hens, so you've got a nice job to do next. And I reckon Jim would have liked my job, sprat though he is! He'd pretend he's got muscles!" She paused, shocked with memory. *I don't know if we'll ever see him again*, she thought.

As if she had heard her, Lizzie burst out, "Why did Ma take him away with her, and leave us behind?"

"How could she leave him here? How could she expect Rosie to help all three of us?" Emily snapped. There came the tears again, sharp as needles behind her eyes. She smiled weakly at her sister. "Do your job, just do it. Let Rosie be pleased with us."

The kitchen was warm again when they went back in. Rosie was trudging up from the cellar with a bucket of coal in each hand.

"I'm going up to light the house fires," she told them. "Luckily, there's only four to do today, as the mistresses are away."

"What shall we do?" Emily asked.

"You could lay his tray for breakfast," Rosie

said. "He has tea, a boiled egg, bread and butter, and marmalade. I've put some aside for us, but we have it when he's done. When you hear Judd coming down you'll have to hide for ten minutes, while she has her breakfast. We have to pretend you're not here, then she can say she knows nothing about you. Silly woman. I think she'll relax a bit once his lordship leaves for work."

Lizzie found the things that were needed for the tray. Emily put the kettle on the hob to boil, and sliced and buttered the bread neatly. When they heard footsteps on the stairs they scrambled into the pantry and waited, breathless, listening to Judd scraping porridge from the pan and slicing herself some bread. They heard Rosie return and Judd giving her orders for the day, and then their door was opened and they stumbled back into the light of the kitchen.

"Breakfast soon," Rosie said. "I don't know about you two, but I'm starving. It's making the fires that does it, lugging ashes down the stairs and coals up. And when the mistresses are here there's even more fires to do."

"What are the mistresses like?" Lizzie asked.

"Well, his wife is as sour as a crabapple and his sister is like a crocodile! Heard of crocodiles? They're all teeth and snap. That's what she's like. They're away visiting relatives in the country, so things are a bit easy just now. But when they get back, I'll be hustled off my feet. And then there's the two Dearies."

"And is there just you and Judd looking after everyone?"

"Lor, do you never stop asking questions?" Rosie gasped. "The Crabapple and the Crocodile have taken their own maids with them. They wouldn't have me or Judd touching their clothes or their hair. Those maids are a hoity-toity pair, and I'm always glad to see them gone. And there's a girl who comes in weekdays to help Judd with the beds and the dusting and polishing upstairs. Judd's training her, but she'll never be much good. She's as lazy as a cat."

"I could do her job!" Lizzie said, but Rosie shook her head. "She's Judd's niece," she mouthed, glancing at the door. "That's how it works in service. Someone speaks for you, and if you get the job, they have to train you and be responsible for you. I was lucky. Your mother spoke for me. She used to buy salmon and shrimps off me for his lordship's supper, and we got to be pals. Like sisters. Oh." She covered her face with her apron and emerged, red-eyed. "How was she to know I couldn't make decent bread for the life o' me!"

One of the bells over the kitchen door jangled sharply, making Lizzie jump.

"That's it," Rosie said. "Time for his lordship's breakfast. Let me see. Bread's done. Tea's done. Tea cosy, marmalade, bread, butter, cup, saucer, spoon, milk, plate, knife. Sugar. Well done, Em'ly love. Tra-la! Open the door for me, Lizzie." She sailed out of the kitchen and up the stairs with the tray, humming to herself.

Emily hugged her sister. "It's all right here," she said. "We're fine for a bit, aren't we?"

"Maybe Ma will be able to come back and fetch us, when she's better," Lizzie whispered. "That's what I want."

But Emily just shook her head, too upset to answer. She looked away, forcing back the sharp sting of tears before she could speak again. "Just try to be happy here, Lizzie. That's what Ma wants for us. I like this big warm kitchen, and all the shiny pots and pans. I like being where Ma used to be when she was well, and doing the sorts of things she used to do, and cooking lovely food. I hope Rosie speaks for me. If I can't be with Ma, and I know I can't, I hope I can stay here."

3

THE TWO DEARIES

Lizzie turned away from her sister and slumped herself down on the bench. She knew Ma had loved this place too. Sometimes she used to bring bits of pie and bowls of stew home, when Judd allowed her to, and told the girls exactly how she had cooked them before she doled out their share. "What's lovely, is cooking with good quality food," she told them. "I can only afford scrag-ends and entrails for us usually, and coarse flour for bread. I do my best to make it taste good – but ooh, it's another world, the way they live at the Big House. I want that for you, girls. Working in a fine big house!"

"I'd prefer to live in one!" Lizzie had said, and they had all laughed because the very idea was so crazy.

But here they were in the Big House, and Emily was doing her best to be as useful and as good a cook as Ma had been. Rosie wanted her to stay –

that was clear. Lizzie bit her lip. *What about me?* she wanted to ask, but daren't. What if Rosie spoke up for Emily and got her a job there? What if Emily could stay, and Lizzie couldn't? What if Rosie couldn't find another job for her? She hardly dared to let herself think about it. What would happen to her, wandering the streets all on her own? She'd rather go to the workhouse. She watched miserably as Emily busied herself tidying away pans, washing Judd's breakfast plates, putting fresh water to boil. She seemed to know exactly what to do here, where things went, how to keep the kitchen neat and clean. She was even humming to herself as she worked. *It's true*, Lizzie thought. *She loves it here. Even though she's crying inside like I am, she's found out how to be a little bit happy.*

At last Rosie came back down carrying the tray. "Look at this! All gone!" she said. "Judd said he didn't say nothing, but he couldn't take his eyes off your bread! His nostrils were twitching as if he was sniffing roses!"

She put the tray down, and Emily took the plates over to the sink immediately to wash them. *Why didn't I think of doing that?* Lizzie wondered.

"He's out for the day soon, so we can breathe clear, but Judd tells me he's bringing a business acquaintance back with him this evening. She's got to show the Lazy Cat how to get a room ready for him, so I'm to do the shopping today. He wants steak and kidney pie for supper. I'll do the meat, cos I love doing that, and Em'ly, you can have a go at the pastry because your ma's was always a dream. Oh, good girl, you've put more water on. Let's have breakfast, and then you and I can go together for the meat, Em'ly. Would you like that?"

"Oh, I would!" said Emily.

Lizzie forced herself to stand in front of Rosie. "What can I do?" she asked timidly.

"What can you do, my love? What *can* you do, that's the trouble. Ah, I know. You can take the Dearies their breakfast. They'll be awake soon. That's a job I hate, and the Lazy Cat can't stand them, but you might like it. It'll cheer them up to see a pretty little girl like you. You can get the tray set now. Tea, bread and butter. Sometimes a bit of marmalade. That's all they ever have."

"How many Dearies are there?" Lizzie asked. She wiped his lordship's tray carefully and reached up to the shelf for clean plates.

"Two of course. His mother and hers."

"What if they tell his lordship about me?"

"They won't," Rosie chuckled. "They forget everything five minutes after it happens, bless them. And even if they did tell him, he'd think they'd made it up."

I'll do it so well, Lizzie told herself, *that Rosie will decide she wants me to do it every day, and she'll speak for me.* She set the tray carefully with china cups and saucers, plates, teapot.

"Shall I do the bread and butter for you?" Emily asked.

"No. I want to do it myself," Lizzie insisted, but Rosie watched anxiously as she sawed at the loaf, tearing off a huge wedge.

"They'll never be able to chew a piece that big. Let me cut it nice and thin for them, and you can have that piece as an extra treat."

Emily started to sweep Lizzie's breadcrumbs up, and Lizzie snatched the broom away from her. "I know how to sweep the floor! I did it yesterday, remember?"

Emily shrugged and caught Rosie's eye. "She's

always like this. Ma used to call her Little Miss Independent."

"And there's nothing wrong with that," Rosie said. "Sisters are s'posed to help each other though, Lizzie. Let brothers do the fighting." They heard the upstairs door closing and saw a pair of feet walking past the window. "That's him gone. It's a wet day, and the streets will be muddy, so his boots will need a jolly good clean when he gets back."

"I'll do them," said Lizzie.

"And they're huge. He's got feet like barges. The Crocodile's the same; always huge, muddy boots to clean, or dusty ones to shine, every single night. Why they can't spend a day in the house and give their feet a rest, I don't know. No, they must go out, whatever the weather." She poured boiling water into the pot and left Lizzie to set milk and sugar next to it. "There you go, Lizzie. There's their bell too, just on time! The Dearies are ready for their breakfast, and breakfast is ready for the Dearies. Up the stairs, turn right, up the next stairs, first door on your left. Don't wash them, Lizzie. That's the Lazy Cat's job, not yours. Come on, Em'ly. We'll catch the butcher nice and early for the best cuts if we hurry."

"Not nervous, are you?" Emily paused as she was picking up her warm cloak, watching Lizzie. She knew how her sister was feeling, with her pale face set in that determined way and her mouth drawn into a thin, tight line. She also knew that Lizzie was determined to do the job as well as she possibly could, for Ma's sake, and that nothing, not even fear of his lordship himself, would stop her. "Good luck, Lizzie," she said. She swung her cloak round her shoulders and followed Rosie out of the door.

Lizzie waited till the sound of their footsteps had gone before she dared to lift up the tray. "Up the stairs, turn right, up the next stairs, first door on my left. No, right. No, left. I'm sure it's left. And I'll do it so well that Rosie will speak for me." She took a deep breath and edged her way out of the kitchen door and up the dark stairs.

Lizzie was so nervous that the cups rattled in their saucers like old bones. The door at the top of the servants' stairs was closed. She lowered the tray down onto the top step and everything tilted dangerously sideways; the cups slid, the cutlery rolled, the tea slurped out of the spout of the pot. She held the tray firm with her shoe pressed against it because the step was so narrow. She didn't want it tipping down the stairs. She turned the knob and pushed open the door, but as soon as she bent down to pick up the tray, the door swung shut again. She tried again, and the same thing happened. She was close to tears. "I could try holding it with one hand, like Rosie does," she thought. "But I might drop it, and then what?" She decided that the only thing she could do was to get herself through the door first. She opened the door, stepped over the tray onto the landing, nearly dislodging it as she did so, and then crouched down so she was wedging the door open with her body. She leaned down, carefully lifted up the tray, and almost overbalanced. She was panting with effort and triumph when at last she managed to stand up and turn round. And there was Judd, arms akimbo, staring at her in amazement.

"What on earth is going on?" she demanded.

The contents of the tray chattered like loose teeth. "I'm taking the Dearies their breakfast."

"Don't you dare refer to them as the Dearies! They're Mistress Rickett and Mistress Whittle. And you're late. Get on with it, keep quiet, and don't go into any room but theirs. Quick!"

A round pasty face appeared from another doorway behind Judd. *The Lazy Cat!* Lizzie thought. *Well, I'll show her how well I can do my job. Better than she can, any day.* Judd stepped away, and Lizzie saw now that the hallway was glowing with colour: flowery wallpaper and carpet, red velvet chairs and curtains, a crystal chandelier gleaming with teardrops like a rainbow. It was not at all like the dingy kitchen down below stairs.

"What are you waiting for?" said Judd. "They won't want cold tea, you know."

The carpet was as soft as grass under Lizzie's feet. At the top of the stairs she paused again. She had completely forgotten which way to go. The first door, but was it on the left or the right? There were six doors on the landing, and all of them were closed. She daren't go back down again, daren't face Judd's wrath and the Lazy Cat's scornful smile. Something told her it would be bad manners to call out. She put the tray down on a polished table and stood outside the first door on the right. *I'm sure it was this one*, she thought. She could hear nothing from inside. She knocked timidly, then more bravely. Still nothing. She turned the knob slowly and peeped inside. In front of her was a bed with a beautiful fringed quilt over it. Standing round the walls were huge pieces of dark wood furniture. There was a standard lamp with a fringed shade, and long, thick green curtains at the windows. But no Dearies. She closed the door softly. Her heart was thumping.

She crept to the door on the other side of the staircase, listened again, and now she could hear the mumble of voices. She knocked softly.

"Knock, knock!" called a voice from inside. "Tea, lovely tea!"

Lizzie opened the door, went back for the tray, and crept into the room. Facing her was a big iron bed with two old ladies sitting bolt upright in it. One had lost her nightcap, and her thin grey hair hung in long strand like cobwebs round her face. She clapped her hands together with delight. "Tea, Mistress Rickett! Tea!"

Mistress Rickett glared at Lizzie with round, pebbly eyes. "Who is it, Mistress Whittle?"

"Please, miss. Please, miss," said Lizzie, glancing from one to the other and trying to bob a curtsy without dropping anything, "I've brought your breakfast."

"Move over, Mistress Rickett," the cobwebby one said. She patted a space clear on the counterpane that covered the bed. "Put the tray down. My mouth's as dry as a desert. Look!" She poked out a yellow tongue.

"Who is it?" Mistress Rickett asked again.

"The tea girl. Pour it out, now! I'm parched."

With shaking hands Lizzie did as she was told. She held out a rattling cup and saucer to each of the Dearies, then stood back, watching them sip their tea. She didn't know whether she was supposed to go or stay. At last Mistress Whittle slurped her way to the bottom of her cup and handed it back to Lizzie.

"Pour me another. Plenty of sugar this time. Put some marmalade on my bread. Poke the fire. Open the curtains. Pour me some more tea." Every so often the orders came, while the two Dearies worked their way through the tea and the bread and marmalade. But worst of all, definitely worst of all, was when the cobwebby one lifted up the counterpane and thrust out her skinny legs.

"Wash us."

"Brush our hair," giggled Mistress Rickett.

"Put us on the commode."

I'll do it, Lizzie thought grimly. Even though she knew it was not her job. *I'll do it so well that Judd will think I'm better than the Lazy Cat.*

At last the Dearies were put back into bed, hair brushed and plaited (which Lizzie quite enjoyed doing), pillows plumped, fire blazing, teapot completely empty, all the bread and marmalade gone. Lizzie had spent all morning with them, and there'd been no sign at all of the Lazy Cat. She could hear her stomach rumbling and realised that she hadn't eaten anything herself yet.

"Is there anything else?" she asked.

"Have you brought tea?" Mistress Whittle asked brightly.

"Who is it?" Mistress Rickett asked. But her eyes were closing, her head sinking back against the pillow. Mistress Whittle looked round at her, tried to nudge her awake, and yawned. She smiled sleepily at Lizzie.

Lizzie tucked the counterpane round them, picked up the tray, and tiptoed out of the room. "Please don't wake up," she whispered. "I'm famished!"

She went quickly down the stairs. No Judd. No Lazy Cat. She opened the door to the servants' quarters and stepped down with a sigh of weary relief. The door swung shut behind her, knocking her so hard that she dropped the tray, sending it and everything on it clattering down the stone steps. Every piece of crockery was broken.

4

LAME BETSY

Emily enjoyed her visit to the butcher's with Rosie. The early drizzle had lifted; the day was blue and sharp. Already the street sellers were singing out their wares: "Fresh watercress!" "Nutmeg graters!" "Pies, all 'ot!" "Muffins and coffee!" Street boys held out their hands: "Spend a penny on a poor boy! No Ma, no Pa! No nuffin'!" Rosie hurried past them all, intent on reaching her favourite butcher's shop before the best cuts of meat had gone. As they drew near the shops, the streets became muddier, churned up by the wheels of carriages and donkey carts. Little sweepers ran in front of the wealthier looking shoppers to clear a path for them through the muck. They didn't bother with Rosie and Emily; they knew they wouldn't be getting any coins from them. Now Emily could see that the gutters were running red with blood. A woman walked past them, bent almost double with a whole sheep slung across her shoulders, heading for the row of butchers' shops. Carcasses of meat hung from the rafters of the shop awnings. The owners, all dressed in butcher's blue, stood outside, shouting out to people to come and buy from "Me, the best butcher in the whole of London town!"

Rosie led the way to the last shop in the row, where the walls were covered in shiny white and blue tiles. Inside, a whistling boy swept the floor clean of blood drips and slopped pieces of fat and bone. Hungry dogs scavenged under the trestles that had been pulled out in front of the shop, and were kicked away by the butcher's hefty boot.

The butcher knew Rosie well, and joked and bartered with her as she talked Emily through the best cuts to buy. He parcelled her purchases up with paper and put them into her basket. "It's people like you who make me a poor man!" he grumbled, as she handed over the coins. "Don't let anyone know I'm selling you meat at this price!"

She turned away, pink-faced and smiling. "He knows I was in the trade myself once," she said to Emily. "Selling whelks and stuff for my granddad. He was so pleased when he heard I'd got a job for his lordship that he gave me a bag of stewing meat for nothing! We'll just get some nice fresh veg now, and we'll have just about done. Back to our baking, Em'ly!"

They hurried on to another stall and chose the vegetables to go with his lordship's dinner. Emily looked longingly at a nearby pedlar's tray of dangling coloured ribbons. *I wish I could buy a lovely red one for Lizzie*, she thought. *One day, when I get some wages, I'll buy her one.* She lifted a strand between her fingers, loving its silkiness and its intense colour of summer poppies.

"Don't daydream, Em'ly," Rosie said. "There's never time for that. Judd will be waiting for me to hand back her purse so she can count out her change. I have to account for every farthing spent, so don't go mooning over bits of ribbon."

"It wasn't for me," Emily said. "For Lizzie. Or Ma." Her voice trembled. She ached when she thought about Ma, all her prettiness gone, thin as a helpless bird that had forgotten how to fly. *Be safe, Ma!*

As soon as they arrived back at the Big House and hung up their cloaks behind the door, Judd flounced downstairs with the Lazy Cat to inspect the meat. She nodded to show she was satisfied, then tipped out the contents of the purse and counted the coins. "You got a bargain," she muttered. "You shop better than you cook, I'll say that for you. Now, before you start the meal, I want logs chopping and more coal fetching to the upstairs fires. The chimney's drawing fast today. We don't need a kitchen girl, Rosie Trilling, we need a fine strong boy. I keep telling Mr Whittle that, but he doesn't want to be told how to spend his money."

Emily's hopes fell. "I can chop wood," she offered, but Judd just snorted. "You're little more than a twig yourself. Rosie's the strong one. She can chop, you can carry, and I want it done now. What happened to the other child?"

And it was at that very moment that Lizzie had dropped the breakfast tray down the stairs. The clatter of china splintering from step to step made all three of them jump like rabbits. Judd pulled open the kitchen door to find a heap of broken china, gobs of butter and cutlery on the bottom step and a heap of crying child on the top one. The Lazy Cat stood behind her, smirking with delight.

"Rosie Trilling, you will pay for the breakages out of your wages," Judd said, very quietly. "And make no mistake about it, these Jarvis girls will have to go."

She lifted her black skirt clear of the mess of broken breakfast remains and swept on up the stairs, followed by her grinning niece. They stepped over Lizzie without even looking at her.

"Come on down," Emily called up to her sister. "I'll sweep up the bits. Come on down, Lizzie."

Lizzie crept down the stairs, hiccupping. She wouldn't look at Rosie. She wouldn't look at Emily, who was still flushed and bright from her visit to the butcher's. She had let them both down. She had let Ma down. She ran past them both and opened the kitchen door into the fluster of the hen yard. The back gate was open ready for a delivery of milk. She ran up the steps and into the road and, blind with tears, straight across the path of the milk cart. The horse reared up in fright, and the woman driving the cart was nearly tipped sideways onto the muddy street.

"Stupid girl! Stupid child!" the woman shouted. "You nearly killed Lame Betsy! And my horse!

You nearly lost me all my milk!"

Lizzie ran on till she came to a row of black railings and clung to it, exhausted and frightened. Behind her, she heard a bird singing in a cage. She remembered now pausing in that very place with Emily and Ma and Jim on their way to the Big House. Was that only yesterday? Ma had told them she was taking them to the only friend she had in the world, to ask for help. She had asked them to be good and they had promised her they would. And what had Lizzie done? She had broken china that Rosie would have to pay for, and she had nearly killed the milk woman.

She sank down and curled herself up with her arms round her knees, not knowing what on earth to do next. Maybe she should find her way to the workhouse, and ask to be taken in. Everybody said it was a terrible place, and that there was no hope left for anyone who went there. But what if Ma had been taken there with Jim? She might find them there, be able to stay with them. Surely that would make it bearable, if they were there. And if she wasn't at the Big House being a nuisance, Judd might take pity on Emily and let her stay on and help

Rosie, and everybody would be happy. How would she get there, and was there more than one? She had no idea. If she stayed here long enough, someone might scoop her up and take her to the workhouse anyway. Or if they didn't, she could beg. She watched a filthy, ragged boy approach a woman, hold out his hand to her, then touch his mouth to show her he was starving. The woman walked past him as if she couldn't see him.

I still haven't had my breakfast yet, Lizzie thought. *But I'm not starving, not like him. Not yet. What must it be like to be like him, to have nobody to look after you, no mother or father, nobody? Nowhere to live? And the streets are full of starving children, that's what people say. Like vermin, they are. Rats.*

She sank her head into her arms. She could hear the whinnying of passing horses, the clop and clap of their hooves. London was busy around her, everyone was going somewhere, but she had nowhere to go. Then she heard a woman's voice, shouting, "Girl! Girl! You!" She looked up, and there was Lame Betsy the milk woman limping across the road, waving her arms to force the carriages to make way for her. She wore a large black boot on one foot, and a much smaller one on the other, and as she walked she dragged the muck of the road behind her with her lame foot. Lizzie scrambled up to dart away, but Lame Betsy grabbed her by the shoulders and forced her to sit down again on the low wall in front of the railings. Then, with a huge harrumphing effort, she sat herself down next to her.

She let her wheezing breath steady a bit, still holding tight to Lizzie's arm to stop her from running off. "I want to know," she said, "why a young girl like you was dashing across the road like that as if she had no eyes to see with and no ears to hear with." She glared at Lizzie. "Seems to me like you're in trouble. Is that right? Really big trouble."

"I am. I broke two cups and saucers, and two tea plates and a teapot."

The milk woman let out a sigh like the *blurt* a horse makes through its nostrils. "And that's enough to make you nearly kill Lame Betsy, is it? And her horse, and yourself? Is it?"

Lizzie shrugged. She thought it probably wasn't.

"So is you running away because you's frightened?"

Lizzie bit her lip. Yes, she had been frightened of

the two Dearies. She was frightened of Judd. She had been terribly frightened when she had dropped the tray down the stairs; she could still hear the echoing shriek and clatter it had made, the terrifying din of shame. But that wasn't everything she was frightened of, and she couldn't find the words to tell Lame Betsy any of it, so she shook her head.

"Let me tell you something. You only run away when things are so bad that you can't go on living in that place no more. I should know. When I was your age I ran away from a dad what beat me, and a ma what drank herself senseless. Is it that bad for you?"

Lizzie shook her head.

"And if you go back to that place, is there no one there what'd be glad to see you? Cos if you just glance over the road, you'll see two people coming along what seems to be looking for someone. There's a cook from a big house who I just happens to know is the kindest person on God's earth, and she's got a person with her who's pretty enough to be your own sister." Lame Betsy let go of Lizzie's arm. "You've got a choice, girl. You can carry on running, or you can go and tell them you're sorry for what you did." She grabbed a railing and hoisted herself up. "Me, I've got to go and find Albert before he trots home all by himself with no milk delivered."

5

WHERE YOU GO, I GO

As soon as Lizzie stood up, Emily spotted her across the traffic of wagons and horses. "She's there, Rosie! She's safe!"

They threaded their way across the road and Emily hugged her sister as if she hadn't seen her for a week; tight, tight, just as Ma used to do. "Never do that again," she whispered. "Never run off without me, Lizzie."

"My word, you gave us a fright. We thought you was lost for good. London is like a maze, girl. We could have been looking for hours," Rosie said. "And, if Judd knows I've left the kitchen without her permission she'll have me hung, drawn and quartered. It's all my fault too. I should never have sent you up to the Dearies. They got you all jittery, I'll be bound. And I should have warned you about that door. I've got the trick of it now, and so has Judd, but it comes shut on you like a charging bull if you don't step out of the way quick enough."

"But I broke all that china, and Judd said you've got to pay for it."

"Poof! They never get given the best china, as Judd well knows, because they've got a habit of chucking it at the wall if the tea's too hot or too cold or too weak or too strong. They must have it just right, or they just hurl it across the room! We keep a good stock in for them and we pick it up cheap in the market when we see it. Come on, girls, let's get back, shall we?"

She hurried away, leaving Emily and Lizzie to try to keep up with her.

"What are the Dearies like, really?" Emily asked. "The dreary Dearies!"

"Ghosts and skeletons!" Lizzie giggled, making her voice wobble. "*Who is it? Give me more tea. Who is it?*" She skipped along, happy now. She was with Emily again, and nobody had told her off for anything. "*More tea!*"

Rosie turned round on her suddenly, her face snapped shut with anger. "Don't you go making fun of the Dearies. They're old, is all, a pair of old dears, and they can't help that. And we'll all be like that one day, even you, if you don't keep barging into cart horses."

Emily clasped Lizzie's hand. "Don't worry about Rosie. She's upset," she mouthed. "She should be busy in the kitchen by now."

They had almost reached the Big House when a smart black and gold carriage drew up close to the main door. A liveried driver jumped down to open the carriage door, and two very tall women climbed out, dusting themselves down and complaining loudly that he had jolted them about like sacks of turnips. Two other women climbed out after them, clutching carpetbags as the driver handed them down from the back.

Rosie turned abruptly and put out her hands to stop the girls from going any further. She lowered her head. "Lor, oh lor, it's the two mistresses. They weren't due back till next week. Don't look at them, whatever you do don't let them notice you," she hissed. "Turn round and go back. Have they gone inside yet?"

Emily risked a quick look over her shoulder. "They're looking at us," she whispered.

"Oh my, I could faint. I could pass out stone cold.

They've seen me now, so I must go on as if I've been on an errand for Judd. That's it. What you must do, you must carry on walking as if you don't know me, and when the mistresses have gone in and the door's shut behind them, run round quick and come in our door. Now scarper."

Emily and Lizzie walked sharply away from her without looking back until they reached the corner. They paused as if they were waiting for someone, and Emily turned her head quickly towards the house. She saw Rosie walk steadily towards the women, bobbing to them as she passed, and then going down the steps to the servants' quarters.

"Why was she so frightened?" Lizzie asked.

"I think she's scared she might lose her job."

"Because of us?"

Emily said nothing, just watched the trundling carts, the bustle of passers-by. The main house door closed, the driver climbed back into his seat and urged his pair of horses to walk on, and still they waited.

"I haven't eaten anything yet," Lizzie said.

Emily nodded. "All right. We'll go in. It should be quite safe now." She began to walk towards the house. "Poor Rosie. Poor Rosie. What have we done to her? If only you hadn't run off like that, Lizzie! What were you thinking of?"

"It was because of yesterday. When Ma left us behind…"

"She had to. You know that. She had no choice."

"Rosie said she'd speak up for you."

"I know."

"But she said she'd take me to her sister's in Sunbury."

"I know."

They had reached the railings of the house. Six steps down, and they would reach the servants' basement. Through the door, and they'd be in the kitchen, and Rosie would be there, and there'd be work to do. There would be no chance of a private talk.

Lizzie grabbed Emily's arm. "You won't let her, will you?" she blurted out. "You won't let her take me away from you?"

"Of course I won't."

"Even if she gets you a job here, and you love it, and it's Ma's kitchen and everything? Even if Judd says you're the very girl she wants?"

"Never," said Emily firmly. She took both Lizzie's hands in her own. "We're sisters, aren't we? Where you go, I go. I promise."

6

SNATCHED IN THE NIGHT

The kitchen was grim with worry. The fire sulked in the grate, there was no sunlight coming through the window; even the pans had lost their sparkle. Rosie was on her hands and knees picking up the last of the shards of broken china. She hoisted herself up and handed Lizzie a small brush.

"Here, you can finish the job. And then you can soap the stairs down."

"I haven't eaten anything yet," Lizzie reminded her timidly.

"Neither have I, neither has your sister. Get that job done first. Em'ly, you can be slicing up some bread and ham for us all. Forget breakfast, as we're long past it now. I couldn't stomach it anyway. Then we've got to get on with cooking that meal for supper. And there's four more to cook for now: the Crabapple and the Crocodile and their two hoity-toities. Good job we bought plenty of meat this morning, Em'ly. And, Lizzie, when you've done the stairs you can take your bread and ham into the pantry. I'm sorry, but you'll have to eat your meal in the dark. I daresay your hand can find its way to your mouth? If the mistresses come down, as well they might, I've got a story for them in my head. But it doesn't include you just at the moment."

An hour later the kitchen was oozing with the smell of juicy meat simmering in a pot over the fire. Emily was rolling pastry, in her quick, light way. She was using the wooden rolling pin that her ma would have worked with. Rosie was chopping carrots and onions. Neither of them spoke a word. Their ears were straining for the sound of Judd's tread on the servants' stairs; and at last it came. The door was flung open, and in she swept, with her black skirts brushing the floury tiles like a duster.

"Rosie, you are to go upstairs – now. Master and Mistress Whittle want to speak to you."

"Yes, Judd." Rosie put down her chopping knife and smoothed her hands clean on the apron. "Have I to take Em'ly with me?" Her breath came out like a trembling shudder.

"Certainly not. They want you on your own.

They want you to explain why you have brought street children into the house."

"Not street children, Judd. Didn't you tell them they're Annie's daughters?"

"They didn't ask me. It's you they want to speak to." Judd swept out of the kitchen, and the flour settled back into the cracks between the stones. Rosie said nothing. She tucked her hair under her cap, removed her working apron and slipped on a newly starched clean one and, without saying a word to Emily, followed Judd up to the main part of the house.

Emily didn't dare to open the door to the larder to see how Lizzie was. She finished rolling the pastry, trying to keep her hands steady, trying to keep the scorch of tears from blurring her eyes. She lined a pie dish with half of the pastry and put it on the windowsill to keep cool, stirred the meat with a wooden spoon, then carried on from where Rosie had left off, chopping vegetables and herbs. Now tears coursed freely down her face, no matter how often she wiped them away.

Rosie came down at last. Her eyes were red. She put her work apron on without saying anything at all.

In silence she transferred the cooked meat from the pot to the pie dish, where it bubbled in its hot gravy. She added the vegetables and herbs and nodded to Emily to roll out the rest of the pastry. She fitted it snugly over the meat, then placed it in the side oven. She raked up the fire. When she spoke at last her voice was flat and dull, and it was only to say that the mistresses would like apple dumplings for dessert, and would Emily be kind enough to show her how to make them as good as her ma did.

All this time, Lizzie was shivering in the dark and cold of the larder, but she wasn't let out until Rosie had made several journeys upstairs with the cooked food and was quite sure that the master and his business acquaintance, and his wife and her sister, the hoity-toities in their attic room and the Dearies in their creaky bed were all tucking into the best meal they'd had for months. A cauldron of water was set above the fire to wash the dishes, and Judd and the Lazy Cat, Rosie, Lizzie and Emily sat down at the kitchen table to eat what was left. Neither Judd nor Rosie said a word.

"Oh la!" the Lazy Cat said. "Trouble!" And was shushed to silence by her aunt's fierce look. Rosie hardly ate a thing, but kept sighing and sniffing and blowing her nose. Emily glanced at Lizzie and shrugged slightly to show her that she hadn't a clue what was going on. She knew Rosie was in trouble, and they thought Judd was probably in trouble too. They also knew that it was all because of them.

Later, when Rosie brought all the dishes down from the various rooms of the main house, she said, simply and flatly, "They ate the lot."

Judd and her niece went upstairs to see to the fires and warm the beds. Rosie looked at the two girls where they sat on the kitchen bench, then briefly put her arms round each of them in turn.

"What's going to happen, Rosie?" Emily asked.

"I want you to get some sleep now. That's what's going to happen next." She gave a long, deep sigh that was full of inner worry. "Like your ma asked, I'm trying to do my best for you. I'm going up to my room. Good night, girls."

Emily and Lizzie lay wrapped in their rugs in front of the fire, watching the flicker of flames as they licked through the damped coals.

"Something bad's going to happen, isn't it?" Lizzie asked.

"I don't know. Ssh now, go to sleep, like Rosie told you. Everything will be all right."

Very soon, in spite of all their worries, the girls fell asleep.

And then, in the middle of the night, Lizzie felt herself being lifted up and carried across the room. She thought at first that it was part of a dream, until the street door was opened and a shock of cold air startled her into wakefulness. She was set down, her cloak put round her shoulders, her boots laced onto her feet and a small bundle thrust into her hands. All this was in the pitch-dark, with no words spoken. Then a hand grasped her own.

"Emily?" But she knew it wasn't Emily's hand; it was too large, too cold, too tight.

"Emily!"

She reached back to the door of the house just as it was closed firmly against her. She heard the key turn in the lock.

"Emily! Emily!" she screamed, and then a hand was clamped across her mouth and she was pulled away, up the steps, and out onto the street.

7

NO CHARITY
CHILDREN HERE

Emily opened her eyes, startled awake. Surely she'd heard Lizzie's voice? She felt across the hearthrug for her, then scrambled to her feet. Lizzie wasn't there! She heard her voice again, footsteps outside, someone running, someone dragging her feet as if she was being pulled along. She groped for the door, helplessly pressing the latch, but it had been firmly locked.

"Lizzie! Lizzie!" She banged on the door with her fists. "Wait for me!"

A light flared behind her, and she turned to see a woman holding up a candle, her nightdress white as a spectre's, her eyes deep and dark in her pale face, her cheeks high and gaunt with deep hollows. Her grey hair hung in long strands round her shoulders.

Emily screamed, and the spectre stepped forward and put a bony hand on her arm. "Hush, girl! Do you want to bring the whole household down here?"

It was Judd's voice. Emily shuddered with relief.

"Please let me out, Judd. Something's happened to Lizzie. I think someone's taken her away."

"Nothing's happened to Lizzie," Judd hissed. "She's with Rosie Trilling."

"She can't be! Not without me!"

"Be quiet! If you must know, Rosie has given up her job. For your sake! You must stop this noise. Upstairs won't take kindly to being woken up in the night by your ranting."

"I don't understand! Rosie wouldn't leave me here. I'm not staying without Lizzie. Let me out!" But Emily could see that Judd had no keys dangling from the waist of her nightgown. Where had she hidden them? She rattled the latch again, helplessly, uselessly.

"Stop that! I think you know very well what I mean. Rosie has been dismissed, to put it plainly. Gone, gone, and taken the girl with her."

"But where've they gone?"

"She's taken Lizzie to try to get her a job in Sunbury with her own sister, and let me tell you that's a long long walk from here, and then it's back home for Rosie, back to an evil grandfather and a wretched life as a coster-girl."

Judd turned to go back to bed, lifting her candle to light her way to the other door, and Emily just caught the glint of something bright in her hand. She knew it was the door key. She ran in front of the housekeeper and tried to snap the key out of her hand. Judd shouted in anger and tried to force her away, and in the tussle she dropped the candle. There came the sound of hurried footsteps on the stairs, the glow of another candle, and a tall woman came into the kitchen. Her hair hung in a long plait over her shoulder, and with one hand she clutched to her throat the ends of a black velvet shawl flung over her nightdress. With the other she held the candle high.

"What in the name of the Lord is going on here?"

Her voice made the pans vibrate on the shelves, the glasses tremble in their locked cupboard, the cutlery jitter in the drawers. Emily recognised her as the older of the two women who had stepped out of the carriage that morning: the Crabapple, mistress of the house. Dithering behind her now were two old ladies, cackling and whooping with excitement, and the Lazy Cat. Her eyes were alight with scorn. "Gone!!" she sighed.

The Crabapple turned to her. "Is this anything to do with you?"

"Not me, no, ma'am. I know nothing about it. Something about two girls who were dragged in from the streets. Friends of that Rosie Trilling. I don't know what they were doing here in your house, ma'am."

The Crabapple advanced towards Emily, thrusting the candle under her face. "Who are you?"

"She's Emily Jarvis. She's the new cook," Judd said, bending to scoop up her candle.

"The new cook?"

"I can cook," the Lazy Cat muttered.

Her Aunt Judd shot her a knowing glance and signalled to her to go back to her room. "Rosie Trilling has gone, like you told her to, ma'am."

"Please don't blame Rosie," Emily begged. "She was trying to help me."

"So we need a new cook," Judd went on. "And this is her."

"The new cook?" the Crabapple said again. "This child?"

"Please, miss, I want to go," said Emily bravely.

"You want to go?"

"She wants to follow her sister," Judd said with a snort, as if it was the most ridiculous idea in the world.

"Then go!" said the Crabapple. "I don't want street girls in my house. Go."

The two Dearies whooped gleefully. The Lazy Cat, lingering in the doorway, smiled to herself.

"Unlock the door, and let her go," the Crabapple said to Judd. "Out, girl. Out. I'll have no charity children here."

Without a word, Judd stalked over to the back door and unlocked it. Emily bundled up the rug she had been sleeping on, snatched her boots, and scampered through the door, across the yard, and up the outside steps to the street.

Below her, the servants' door was slammed shut and locked.

8

ALONE

Dawn was beginning to break with a grey, steely light. The street was deserted, except for the lamplighter tramping towards the main road, stretching up his long pole to extinguish the street lamps. Emily ran to him, her bare feet slapping the cold stones.

"Wait, oh wait! Please, mister, have you seen a woman and a girl coming this way?" she panted.

Saying nothing, the lamplighter just pointed to where an early mist was coiling up in smoky wreaths from the direction of the river. Emily ran on to the Thames and along the bank, calling, "Lizzie! Lizzie! Lizzie!" She had to find her. Would they have gone this way, or that? "Lizzie! Rosie!" Her voice echoed off the old boat sheds. People were beginning to move, horses were being fastened to their carts, beggars uncurling from their sleeping-holes. Costermongers trudging out of their cottages, their trays loaded with breakfast shrimps to sell to the early-morning workers; street children crept like rats out of the shadowy arches of bridges to scavenge what they could. But there was no sign of Lizzie and Rosie.

"Which way? Oh, which way?" Emily gazed round in despair.

"'Ere. You're lost, ain'tcha?"

A boy was sitting in the gutters, with a string of shoelaces in his hand. He was dressed in the tattered clothes of a street child, barefoot and dirty, with tangled hair.

"Don't know yer way back home? Cos like, I know these streets inside out and upside down, I do, and I can take you anywhere you wants to go, and maybe your ma and pa would give me a penny or a farving for finding you, or maybe not, I don't care." He grinned up at her. "Why don't you sit down for half a minute and catch your breff, and have a little fink?"

She shook her head, though she was exhausted with running so far. She didn't have time to take a rest. Rosie was a quick walker. They could be anywhere by now. "I'm looking for my sister," she said. "And my friend Rosie. You haven't seen them, have you?"

The boy frowned. "Not seen no one this morning of the female kind, 'cept for Raggedy Annie and the like. Seen a lot of dogs. There was an old man as wouldn't buy me laces, even though his own was frayed like pieces of old straw. Too mean, he was, and when he trips over he'll remember me and fink, I wish I'd helped that boy out. But I ain't noticed anyone else this morning. Why don't yer go back home? Maybe they'll be there, waiting for you."

Emily shook her head, too upset to speak now. She turned away from him and began to trudge back the way she had just come. She hadn't got a home, not any more. Even if she found her way back to the Big House, she couldn't go inside. She didn't belong there now. She didn't belong anywhere. She felt a surge of panic. What if she didn't find them? What on earth would she do?

"Any idea where they was heading?" the boy called after her.

She stopped. "Yes!" Why hadn't she thought of that? She tried to force the word out of the back of her memory. Somewhere that made her think of sunshine. "Sunbury! They were going to Sunbury!"

He whistled softly. "That's out of my patch, that is. Cor, it's miles and miles away! Tell you what. You'll have to get onto one of the main roads and ask the coachmen there. Go along there to that big church and then you'll find some coaches. Maybe they've took one, cos they won't be walking that far I don't fink."

"They won't be on a coach," Emily said sadly.

The boy whistled again. "No money, eh? There's only two choices for people wiv no money. The streets, or the workhouse up that lane, and I know which one I choose. I've been there, I have, and I got out again as quick as a cat. Never go there again, I won't."

Emily started running again. Her head was thudding. She'd wasted too much time; she shouldn't have stopped. She must have really lost them by now. Ahead of her she saw the church. She could just make out a line of coaches where someone might tell her the way to Sunbury. Sunbury – the long, long walk. Could Lizzie manage it? But what were the other choices? The streets, and a life of begging and stealing and sleeping under bridges. Would Rosie let that happen? The workhouse. No, no, not the workhouse. Surely they wouldn't go to the workhouse. But Ma might be there. Jim might be there. She stood at the end of the lane that the boy had pointed to. At the far end, she could see a tall building with black gates. No. They wouldn't go there. Never.

9

MRS CLEGGINS

Rosie and Lizzie had stopped running by now. They were well away from the Big House, and Rosie knew that Lizzie would never find her way back there on her own. She drew her under a bridge to rest a little, and let go of her grasp. Gulls screeched mournfully, the tide was out, the riverbanks were a stinking mess of mud and fish bones and rubbish. Further down the river they could see a huddle of fishermen's cottages, clustered together like a mouthful of rotting teeth.

"That's where I come from," said Rosie. "That's where I was born. Went up in the world, I did, thanks to your ma." *And now it looks as if I'm sunk back down, just like that*, she thought to herself.

Lizzie thought the cottages looked even worse than Mr Spink's tenement house where she used to live with Ma and Emily and Jim. How long ago was that? Only three days? And where was Ma now? Where was Jim?

"Is that where you're taking me?"

"Oh no. My granddad would eat you up. Like a snappy dog, he is. He's wicked. I wouldn't take you there. No, Lizzie, we're going to Sunbury."

"I want to go back to Emily. Back to the Big House."

"Well, you can't," Rosie said firmly. "We've been kicked out. There, now you know, and I wasn't going to tell you that. We've got to go to Sunbury, or starve, and that's the truth. It's our only hope now. My sister might speak for us. We'll be all right there, maybe. But we're going to be walking till our legs drop off, so best get a move on. Up that lane now."

It was beginning to drizzle with a sharp, frosty sleet. Rosie stopped to pull her shawl up over her head. *I wish I was back in that big warm kitchen*, she thought. *The job of my dreams, that was, working there. Never again, Rosie. Not for you.*

"What's that big building up there, with the black railings?" Lizzie asked. She had a feeling that she knew very well what it was, that it had been pointed out to her in the past as a house to be afraid of, a last-place-in-the-world sort of house, more frightening even than a graveyard.

"It's the workhouse," Rosie said. She tugged Lizzie's arm, anxious to hurry past the place, but Lizzie pulled herself away from her.

"I want to go there. If I can't go back to the Big House, I want to go there."

"Not there! I won't let you."

"But Ma might be there. And Jim. I want to be with them." Lizzie was already running up the middle of the slippery road, and all Rosie could do was to lift her skirts out of the muck and run after her. *Maybe*, she thought fleetingly, *it would be for the best*. In her heart of hearts she knew that her sister would never be able to find work for both of them, probably not even for one of them. At least if Lizzie was in the workhouse she would have food of sorts, and a roof over her head. She wouldn't be sleeping on the streets like the other homeless children. But the nearer she drew to the huge iron gates that kept the inmates of the workhouse away from the rest of the world, the more her dread and fear of the place grew.

Never, she thought. *I'll never let Annie's child go there.*

Lizzie had nearly reached the railings when she

saw a group of children being herded out of the door into the workhouse yard. A boy ran ahead of the others and stood clutching the railings with both hands, his white face peering out through the bars.

"Jim! It's Jim!" Lizzie yelled, slipping down on the greasy cobbles in her eagerness to get to him. But when the boy turned his head to look at her she could see that it wasn't her brother at all. He stuck his hand through the bars.

"Got any bread, miss? Got some cheese?"

"Do you know Jim Jarvis?" Lizzie asked him. "Did a boy come here with his mother, and she was sick and weak and he probably had to help her to walk – did you see them?"

The boy looked puzzled. "A boy and his ma?"

"Did you see them? She's Mrs Jarvis. Annie." Lizzie looked over her shoulder anxiously. Rosie had nearly reached her. "He's called Jim. He's my brother."

"Jim Jarvis?" the boy repeated. "Jim Jarvis and his ma?" As if it was part of a nursery rhyme that he was trying to remember.

As soon as Rosie reached them she fumbled in her bag and brought out a hunk of cold pastry that she had saved from last night's supper. It was meant to keep them going on their long walk to Sunbury. She held it out towards the boy and as she did so, she shook her head very slightly, and narrowed her eyes, and made her mouth into the silent shape of "no".

"No," said the boy quickly. "No Jim Jarvis here." He snatched the crust and ran to join the other children who were being hustled towards the gates by the ancient workhouse porter.

"Stand 'ere and wait till the coach comes," the old man was saying to them. "And thank the Lord you're going to a better life. Is that Tip?" he shouted to the boy. "What you eating? Been beggin', 'ave yer?" He grabbed the boy and dragged him away. "You 'eard what Mr Sissons said! Wait nice and quiet till Mrs Cleggins comes. No begging, no annoying, be'ave like a gentleman! Lost yer chance now, you fool." And he dragged Tip back inside the workhouse building. The other children clustered together, giggling nervously. A tall, handsome boy grinned and raised his hand as if he was saluting as a smart carriage drew up to the gates. The waiting children cheered and surged forward.

"There you are," said Rosie. "They're not there,

and nor will you be. It's no place to live or die, I can tell you that."

"No, it's not," Lizzie agreed. She looked at the grim, soot-blackened building and shuddered, and then turned her back on it. "I don't want to go there. Not if Jim and Ma aren't there. Not ever."

"Lizzie!" a familiar voice shouted. "I'm here! I'm here!"

But it wasn't Jim's voice, or Ma's. It was Emily, running up the lane from the river. "Don't go without me!"

"Oh lor!" sighed Rosie. "Two of them now!"

"I told you I wouldn't let you go," Emily gasped, panting up to them. "I ran and ran, and I didn't know where to look for you, and then I thought, the workhouse, that's where they'll be, and I was right."

"Don't tell me you've quit that good job," Rosie said. "Now what?"

"I don't care what happens now," Emily said. "As long as I'm with Lizzie."

"Are these girls for me?" a sharp voice called. Rosie looked round to see that a hefty, ruddy-faced woman was leaning out of the carriage window. "Homeless girls?"

"I suppose they are," Rosie sighed. "Why do you want to know?"

"Because I'm looking for a pair of strong, healthy girls just like these two." The woman had a strange, flat accent that was a bit difficult to understand. Lizzie watched her, fascinated, and the woman caught her eye. Her mouth twitched into a grim sort of smile that showed her brown teeth. "Got their papers? Indentures?"

A wagon drew up behind the carriage. "Get in, children," the woman shouted to the waiting huddle, and with great excitement the children from the workhouse all climbed in.

"And you two." The woman nodded to Emily and Lizzie. "You can send their papers on. I'm in a hurry."

"Wait a minute," Rosie said. "Who are you? Where are you taking these children?"

"I'm Mrs Cleggins," the teeth clacked. "Of Bleakdale Mill. I'm here to collect homeless children, *good* homeless children, from workhouses and streets. I look after them, poor little mites. I give them a future! I have plenty of work for them."

"What kind of work?" Rosie asked suspiciously.

But her heart was beginning to lift.

"They'll be apprentices. Out of kindness of his heart, Mr Blackthorn gives apprenticeships to poor and needy children They're all going to learn to be textile workers. He gives them a new life! You're very lucky, I've got room for these two today. I think in the circumstances and out of charity Mr Blackthorn will overlook the lack of proper documents. I were promised ten lads and ten lasses from this workhouse, but looks like there's only eight lasses here." She clacked her teeth together impatiently, then added as an afterthought, "Probably too sick or died, poor creatures. A life in country might have saved them. Don't tell me you don't want these lasses to come!"

"I don't know," Rosie said doubtfully. "I promised their mother I'd look after them."

"Well, they'd have a lovely life with me. Fresh country air, good country food, and a job for life. Make your mind up, I can't dally all day."

"They'd get a wage, would they?"

"Naturally. And clean clothes. Oh, put them inside wagon. They're hardly dressed for this rain. I cannot bear to see them shivering like that."

"I don't know what to say." Rosie turned away.

"What do you think, girls?"

Emily sensed the despair in Rosie's voice. "Maybe we could go there just for a bit, Lizzie, till Rosie finds somewhere for us all to live."

"Would it be like when we used to live in the cottage, before Pa died?" Lizzie asked. "Would we have a cow and a pig?"

"I think your lasses want to come," Mrs Cleggins said.

"Do you really?" Rosie asked them. Her heart was fluttering. *I've no job, I've no home, I've nothing to give them*, she thought. *What right do I have to deny them a promising future like this?*

"It's not fair to expect Rosie to look after us both," Emily whispered to Lizzie. She squeezed her sister's hand. "We'll try it," she said.

Rosie made a choking sound like a strangled cough in her throat. She fumbled inside the bundle she was carrying and thrust something towards Lizzie. "Here, I made this rag doll for my sister's child. Have it, to remember me. God bless you both."

She hugged them quickly and then hurried away so she didn't have to watch them clambering into the wagon. She heard the doors being slammed shut behind them, heard the driver yelling coarsely to the horses to "Gerra move on, will yer!" and the snort and rumble as the carriage and wagon moved away. She turned then, one hand lifted in a wave of farewell, the other clasped to her mouth.

"There you are, Annie. I've done my best for your girls. Just like I promised."

10

WE'RE GOING TO A
MANSION, REMEMBER?

It was dark in the wagon now the doors were closed, with just a piercing of daylight where ropes had been slashed into the canvas to make a roof. The floor was covered with straw, which the workhouse children were flinging about excitedly.

"We'll have our own horses to ride!" A girl about Lizzie's age draped a mane of straw across her bubbly curls. "Neigh! Neigh!"

"Don't be daft, Bess," said an older boy. "All you'll get is a donkey!" He smirked down at her as all the other children laughed. "But I'll have a big black stallion!"

"We'll have roast beef and pudding every night," another boy chuckled. He grinned at Emily. "Ever had roast beef before? I haven't!"

"Roast beef and pud, if you're very, very good!" the other children chanted.

"That's what Mr Sissons told us," Bess said to

Lizzie. "He was the Beadle at the workhouse, and we'll never ever have to look at his spiky old chin again."

"I'm so happy, I could burst!" the chuckly boy said. "This is the best day of my life this is, and no mistake. I didn't know what happy was, till now."

"Smiley Sam!" Bess giggled. "That's you now, ain't it? We're all smiling now, ain't we! Even Robin!" She pointed to the handsome boy who wanted a black stallion. "Robin Small, 'e knows it all. Robin Small, 'e's very tall!" she laughed. "Robin Small, 'e rules us all!" She flung a heap of straw at him and it showered over his face like strands of gold.

Emily and Lizzie sat back to back, propping each other up as the wagon swayed along the streets. Soon the excitement of the released workhouse children began to simmer down as they crouched together to make themselves more comfortable. After they left London the lanes became stony and bumpy, and they were jostled and thumped against each other like sacks of potatoes. It was funny at first, but then a thin child called Lucy was sick. Emily thought she was going to be sick as well. She slumped down with her hands over her face, moaning. However much

Bess and the other children shouted to the driver to stop for a bit, they were ignored. Most of them spent the rest of the day's journey crouched on the floor of the wagon, retching and wretched. Only Bess stayed cheerful, reminding them about the beautiful big house they were all going to live in soon, in the countryside.

At last the wagon stopped for the night. It was pitch-dark by then. The children were allowed out one by one to relieve themselves round the back of a wayside hostel. Emily thankfully breathed in the cold night air and stood gazing up at the sparkle of stars and the moon that blazed like a carriage lamp.

"Feeling better now?" Sam asked her. "Ain't it grand! Grand!"

Lizzie and Bess were both asleep, but were ordered to be "Up and out with yer!" by a stable lad who'd been told to clean out the straw in the wagon and replace it with fresh.

"I wanted a job like that, when I was little," Sam said wistfully. "My dad was a stableman, and I used to help him. Love horses, I do. But now – I'm going to be a 'prentice! Even better! Grand, that is!" He swung his arms backwards and forwards, trying to warm himself. Emily clutched her cloak tighter against the nibbling wind.

"Anyone hungry?" the innkeeper called. He limped to the wagon carrying a big pot, and set it down in the yard. "Here's some mutton stew for you, out of my own goodness. I'm sorry for you lot, and no mistake. You've got at least four more days of travelling like this. The lanes will turn to tracks and the horses will go lame before you get where you're going. And when you get there, you're in for a hard life. Still, you're young."

He limped away, leaving the children clustered together, cold and silent and afraid now. All the excitement of the morning had fizzled away. A boy ran out from the inn with an armful of wooden bowls, which he flung to the ground in a clattering heap. One of the older girls, Miriam, took it on herself to ladle out the broth. Lizzie crouched next to Emily, warming her hands round her bowl.

"I wish we hadn't come," she muttered.

"So do I. I wish Rosie had just left us at the workhouse gates, and we'd have gone in and lived there."

"Don't you ever say that!" Miriam said. "Never, ever say you wished you were in the workhouse. I'd rather travel like this for a month, and be sick every day of it, than have one more night in that place."

"Fings'll get better, you'll see!" Bess chimed in. "That old man knows nuffin'! We're going to a mansion, remember?"

But the innkeeper was right about the journey at least. The children lost count of the days and the nights; it seemed that they would live for ever in darkness, lying on prickly straw, jostled together till they were bruised all over. For the final part of the journey they had the impression that the wagon was going down a long, steep slope, lurching and plunging and threatening to topple over. They could hear the driver whipping the horses and cursing them for only having four legs each, and just when they all, even Sam and Bess, thought that the world was about to end, the wagon came to a juddering halt.

"We're here! We're here at last, and I'm never doing that miserable journey again!" the driver bellowed. "Get out, and be thankful you didn't end up in the water."

An icy wind shrilled through the wagon as the back

doors were hauled open, and the children stumbled out. Lizzie clutched Emily's hand, frightened by the din of furious water. A river gushed and swirled nearby, drowning out everything except the high-pitched shriek of the wind. The moon shone like a huge blinking eye through the racing clouds, lighting and shadowing the great flank of black hills that surrounded them, seeming to press down on them on all sides. In the distance, they could just make out the massive bulk of a building with hundreds of blank eyes set into it.

A woman approached, walking head-down into the wind, lantern held her to light her way over the rough ground. With her free hand she held down her black skirts, which were flapping round her ankles like the wings of an untidy crow. She perked her face up as she approached them, and they recognised her as Mrs Cleggins, who must have travelled much faster than them in her comfortable coach. Saying nothing, she gestured to the children to follow her. They picked up their little bundles, hugging them with their arms folded across them because they were the only things they possessed in the world. Lizzie had Rosie's rag doll and a grey dress, wrapped round in a blanket. Emily had a woollen rug. Everything else they possessed had been left at the Big House, and probably had been thrown out by now.

They all trudged silently after Mrs Cleggins. She opened the door of a large white building, and counted the children as they passed through. As soon as she closed the door the howl of the wind and the rushing sound of the river softened down, though the shutters rattled and the candle flames fluttered like dry leaves, and in the hearth, a crackling fire hissed and spat. A hefty woman with freckled skin was sorting out piles of clothes at a long table. There were rows of wooden desks and benches in the room, and Mrs Cleggins told them all to sit down. She stood with her back to the fire.

"This is the apprentice house," she said, in her strange, flat accent. "And I am mistress of it. You do everything what I tell you. You do nowt wi'out asking me. Lasses' bedroom is upstairs, lads' on floor above that. You may only go to them to sleep in. Rest of time will be spent here in school room, or working at mill."

"Please, miss?" Bess interrupted.

Mrs Cleggins's mouth stayed open for a long

moment then clacked shut again. She ignored Bess. "You will begin work at six. At eight you will have your breakfast. Skivvy will bring it to you at your machine. You'll have your dinner at one. You get half an hour, so you eat it at machines or out in yard if you can stand weather."

"Will it be roast beef?" Bess asked.

"Roast beef? Who on earth promised you roast beef?" Mrs Cleggins's eyes narrowed into slits.

"Big boys at the workhouse." Bess turned round, waiting for the others to agree. No one spoke. "Didn't they? Sam, you remember! They said we'd have roast beef for dinner."

Mrs Cleggins stood with her hands on her hips. A flicker of smile ghosted across her face and disappeared as if it had never been. "Have you ever had roast beef, lass?"

Bess shook her head.

"Well then, roast beef is what you'll get. Only up here we call it porridge." Her shoulders shook with silent laughter. "After dinner you return to work. At six you finish work and return here for your tea. You will have one hour of hymn practice and Bible readings. Then you will go to bed."

"But, miss," Bess interrupted her again. "When do we ride our horses?"

The handsome boy, Robin Small, tittered.

"Your *horses*!" repeated Mrs Cleggins, astonished. "*Horses?*"

There was complete silence in the room. That was when the children knew for certain that the innkeeper had been right. Life would not be better here. There were no horses for them, no roast beef, no fine clothes. The mansion was this bare, cold apprentice house.

"Open up your bundles for inspection. I'll collect up clothes you've been sent with," she continued. "You won't need those till Sundays. Skivvy will give you your work clothes in a minute." The hefty woman grinned gummily round at them. "Blue frocks, white caps and aprons for lasses; wool trousers, blue shirts and caps for lads. Clothes you're wearing will stand for Sunday spares. Give me your boots. You'll be wearing clogs from now on." Mrs Cleggins swept up and down the rows, collecting all the clothes and boots into baskets. She nodded at Lizzie to drop her doll into the pile. "No need for dolls. You're a working lass now. An apprentice. Of course, you don't have any indenture papers, you two. I remember you. I shall have some explaining to do to Master Blackthorn. How old are you? "

"Nine," Lizzie whispered.

"You don't look it, but it's as well if you are, or I'd have to lie. He's not allowed to employ under-nines no more. And your sister doesn't look much older."

"Please, miss, what's an indenture?" Emily asked.

"It's papers what says you're bound as an apprentice here for next seven years, that's what an indenture is." Mrs Cleggins snapped her teeth together and moved on. Lizzie looked at Emily, alarmed. She counted on her fingers. Seven years! Till I'm sixteen!

When she'd filled up the baskets, Mrs Cleggins stood at the front of the room again, with her back to the fire.

"You can wash yourselves out in yard now. Pump is at back. Then put on your work clothes and give your old clothes to Skivvy."

"But it's dark," Lizzie whispered to Emily, and Mrs Cleggins was suddenly there, leaning across the desk towards her, eyes as sharp as pins.

"Aye, it's dark, but it's morning dark, not night dark. Get washed and changed and no mithering." She stood up again. "Just for this morning, Skivvy will give you your breakfast porridge before work. But be quick with your washing or you'll get nowt."

The children washed themselves and changed out of their old clothes into the stiff, heavy millworkers' shirts and dresses. The girls were shown how to pull back their hair under their white caps, and given long aprons with sleeves. "You'll work and sleep in them," Skivvy told them. "So keep them dry, or you'll catch your deaths. Your cloaks for cold days are upstairs, but you won't be given them today. Not till it's freezing, or church days."

When they were all dressed she brought in the porridge cauldron. She stirred it round with a wooden spoon and beamed at them, showing her pink gums. "Good and ready," she crooned. "Hold out your hands. Right hand!" Into each child's outstretched hand she slapped a ladleful of cold porridge. "This is how you'll get it at your machines, so you might as well get used to it. When you've eaten up, wipe your hand on your clothes. That's it."

They heard a clattering on the stairs as more

children came down from their rooms, yawning and stretching, staring sleepily at the new apprentices. Mrs Cleggins gave one of them a lantern and shooed them all outside. Then she turned to the new arrivals.

"Have you done? Follow me down to mill now and you'll be given your jobs. Line up. Small ones at front." She grasped Lizzie and Bess by their shoulders, frowned at Emily and then pushed her with them. Then she led them to the door, and beckoned to the others to line up behind them. "You'll be under Crick – and watch him, he's got a right nasty temper has Crick. Put your clogs on. Bigger children line up at back."

Miriam caught hold of Emily's arm and pulled her with her to join the queue for the clogs, which were heaped up by the door.

The door was pushed open suddenly and a man stood there, tall and stern, blocking the way out. He glared round at the shivering, sleepy children.

"Is this what you brought me, Mistress Cleggins? This skinny lot? Is this the best you could do?"

"They're hard-working, Mester Crispin. I can promise you that," the woman said.

"I'll be watching you all," he growled. "You've

been given the best chance of your lives, coming to be apprentices at father's mill. He's the owner; I'm the boss. Remember that!"

"Yes, mister," the children murmured.

The big man scowled and turned away into the cold, dark morning, leaving behind him a thrill of horror.

"Is that Crick?" Bess whispered. "He's got a big voice, ain't he? Like a cow."

"That was Mester Crispin, son of mill owner," Mrs Cleggins said. "Never do anything to make him angry, or you'll know about it. Never give my apprentices a bad name, any of you. Now, you big lads" – she nodded at Robin and some of the other taller boys – "you go to the very back. That's it. You'll be in spinning sheds, all of you big 'uns. Little'uns'll be scavenging, rest'll be piecing. You'll find out. Overlookers will tell you what to do, and you'd better do it or you'll get slapped right smart. Out, out now. Follow other lot. Quick, quick, quick. Dawdlers get strap, late-comers get pay docked. Go!"

11

BLEAKDALE MILL

Bess grabbed Lizzie's hand. "Let's run together. I'm excited to start work, aren't you? And we'll get wages to spend every week! I never thought it would happen to someone like me. Are you excited too?"

"A bit." Lizzie looked up at the deep blackness that was the side of a hill, and saw golden lights, all in a line, dipping and bobbing down towards their track. A strange muffled clapping came with it, and then the lights became lanterns and the clapping became clogs and the mill workers from the village over the hill surged onto the track, bringing the morning star with them.

"They sound like horses!" giggled Bess. "So there are horses here, after all!"

The apprentices were being rushed along, swept up in the tide of muttering and panting and coughing mill workers. Lizzie looked round to find Emily, but her sister was lost in the crowd. The great mill building loomed towards them, every window glowing with candlelight. A massive wooden wheel turned against one of the walls, churning water into its buckets. From inside the building came an unearthly racket, and when the doors were flung open and the workers and apprentices swarmed inside, the noise became deafening. The ground floor was a whirl of big moving machines, huge bales of cotton, men stripping off shirts as they set to work in the steamy heat. Lizzie and Bess hurried past them with the other apprentices and on up winding stairs that rang with the sound of their clogs, and up again, across an echoey passage and out into the spinners' floor. Lizzie still held tight to Bess's hand. She had no idea where Emily was now.

In front of them were long rows of machines that rattled, rumbled, thundered; that seemed to be alive, to have arms and fingers and elbows thrashing ceaselessly backwards and forwards. The workers streamed towards them, replacing the people who had been on night shift so smoothly that the machines never stopped, and the day workers bent to their jobs, staring steadily at the threads of cotton that were winding and stretching and pulling on the dancing spindles. Cotton fluff floated everywhere, like wisps of snow, slow and delicate and beautiful amid all the frightening sounds and movement. There was a rank, oily smell that Lizzie could almost taste. She put her hands over her nose and mouth. Bess put a finger in each ear and grinned round at her, shouting something that couldn't be heard.

A man wearing a tall black hat came towards them and grabbed each of them by the shoulder. He jerked his head to where workers were piling their clogs by the door, and Lizzie and Bess did the same. Lizzie just caught sight of Emily then, as she was being led to the end of the room with some of the other girls. They exchanged brief, scared glances. The man bent down to Lizzie and cupped her face. Two fingers were missing from one of his hands.

"Don't dawdle. Get moving," his lips seemed to say, though she couldn't hear his voice at all. His mouth was a wide hole opening and shutting like a blinking eye. She could see his yellow tongue; what teeth he had were black, twisted stumps. *He must be Crick*, Lizzie thought. *The one with the right nasty temper*. She saw now that he had a whip tucked under his arm. He jerked Lizzie and Bess through the long rows of machines. The spinning frames seemed to stretch for ever, with men, women and children busy working at them, wrapped in a trance of concentration.

Crick stopped by one of the machines, which was being operated by a woman who reminded Lizzie of Rosie, big and untidy with sandy hair sprawling out from under her cap and around her wide, smiling face. The overlooker pointed to a small boy who was squirming on his hands and knees under the frame of the machine. Lizzie watched, horrified, as the rattling carriage of the machine passed steadily backwards and forwards over the boy's head. When it was directly over him he flattened himself on the floor, then when it made its journey back he scrambled out from under it with a fistful of cotton fluff, which he crammed into a sack; then again, timing his scramble to a split second so he dived under the machine carriage just in time for it to miss his head as it moved forwards again. He crouched right to the back of the machine, so it was as if he was inside a cage of spars and threads, all trembling with noisy energy. When he squirmed out again he pattered down to a spot further along the spinning mule and dived down under it. Crick pointed to Lizzie, pointed to the boy, and laughed.

"Me? No, I couldn't do that! Please don't make me?" Lizzie begged, pulling away from him, but Crick pressed his hands on her shoulders and forced her to crouch down, and down again, till she was on her hands and knees on the floor. Then he pushed her head down and shoved her under the machine with his boot. She could hear it thudding and hissing above, like a beast bearing down on her. Terrified, she tried to squirm back out, but Crick had his foot pressed firmly behind her. Abruptly he hauled her out and lifted her upright by the neck of her frock.

"If you're any slower than that, you'll lose the top of your head," he mouthed at her. Then he pulled Bess away to scavenge under a different row of spinning mules.

The woman who was working the mule shook her fist behind his back. "Get down now!" she mouthed, and Lizzie crouched to all fours, trembling. She felt a light touch at her back and scurried under the machine, her eyes shut tight, her head tucked down as low as she could get it, then she felt a touch of a foot against her heel and she squirmed back out again. The woman nodded to her to do it again, and then again.

"Now go in further, much further," the woman mouthed. "Listen to my mule. You'll hear when to back out again."

Lizzie ducked in again. She squirmed under the machine as far as she dared, then flattened herself out so she could reach right to the very back of it. She could hear and feel the intense vibration of the mule as the carriage rolled back again. Trembling and sick with fear, she backed out into the aisle. The woman grinned at her and pointed to Lizzie's fist. It was empty. She had completely forgotten to pick up any lint. *But at least I've still got a head, and all my hair,* she thought. *I did it!*

She risked a look round to see where Bess was, but there were too many machines, too much bustle and movement. She could see Crick's black hat, and then the man himself, striding along the aisles. He never took his eyes off the machine workers; from time to time he would cuff one of them on the cheek. She saw him drag the little scavenger boy out from under one of the machines at the far end of her aisle and shake him as if he was made of rags, then drop him on the floor. His mouth was opening and closing like a barking dog's. There was cruelty in his face and his eyes, in the twist of his mouth, in the way he walked, in everything about him. He turned to come down Lizzie's aisle and she ducked quickly under the frame. She would have liked to stay there, hiding from him, but she knew how dangerous that would be. When she wriggled out again she could see his black studded clogs, waiting for her. She stood up and opened up her fist to show him the bunch of fluff she had grabbed. He nodded to her to drop it into the sack and walked on, swishing his cane.

By the time the skivvies came round with their cauldron of breakfast porridge Lizzie felt as if she had been scavenging for days. Her back was aching from bending and squirming, but she knew that she must never stop. She was too afraid of Crick to do that. She had to keep moving up and down the long machine; her feet were as tired as her back. Her head was thumping, and she felt sick with the smell of grease and the heat of the shed. The workers didn't leave their machines or stop to eat. They ate their porridge from one hand and continued working, and wiped the slimy hand clean on their clothes when they had finished, just as Skivvy had shown them that morning.

Flo, the spinner on Lizzie's machine, grinned at her cheerfully. "You all right?" she mouthed.

"I can't see my sister," Lizzie said.

Flo shrugged and waved her hand. There were dozens of workers, dozens of aisles, dozens of whirring machines. Emily could be anywhere.

12

WHAT KIND OF LIFE?

When Emily ran up the stairs that morning, a large woman next to her cupped her hands round her mouth and shouted, "You a new apprentice?"

Emily nodded.

"You stick with me then. I need a piecer on my machine. I had a lad, but he lost his hand last week. Terrible, that was. You have to watch these machines every second, don't take your eyes off them or you'll be hurt bad. I'm Moll. I'll sort you out." She nodded to the overlooker and pointed at Emily. "She's with me," she mouthed and the man waved his hand at her to carry on. Emily noticed then that everyone was lip-reading things to each other, pulling strange faces and opening their mouths wide to make conversation even when they couldn't be heard. Some of the women seemed to be telling each other jokes in a comical mime of hand movements and exaggerated widening of eyes and grimaces, and then bending over in soundless laughter. When the overlooker saw them he would tap them smartly on the shoulders to get on with their work, and they would pull faces at him as soon as he passed.

Emily could have watched them all day, fascinated, and trying to interpret what they were mouthing to each other, but Moll yanked her arm and led her to one of the machines.

"My baby," she mouthed with a wink, and Emily smiled at her, too shy to attempt to mouth anything back. The woman operating it glanced up, gave a weary smile, and slipped away, untying the belts of her apron and yawning; her long working night was over. Moll jerked her head to indicate that Emily must watch her hands. She leaned across the moving bed of the machine to repair any threads of cotton that had broken or twisted in the spindles.

"You've to mind all these spindles." Moll cupped her hand round Emily's ear and yelled instructions down it. "And there's a hundred of them, so work fast! Thread's always breaking and you must mend it as quick as a flash, or it gets tangled up and machine stops and you get bashed and I lose my wages." Up and down she walked, eyes skimming the threads, bending, stretching, snatching as the spindles moved endlessly backwards and forwards, backwards and forwards. Eventually Moll nodded and moved further along the machine, leaving Emily to it while she carried on with her own job. Now Emily had the whole length of the machine to cover on her own. She gritted her teeth, trying desperately to concentrate as the whirring spindles moved towards her and away from her, forwards and away in a wild spinning frenzy. She was too small for the job; she found she had to stand on her toes to reach some of the threads, so she swayed dangerously near the machine. She was tired from lack of sleep, and still aching from being thrown about in the wagon for days on end. She was hungry too; that scoop of porridge that the skivvy had given her had slid off her hand onto the floor, and she hadn't been given another one. But most of all she was worried. What kind of life had she brought Lizzie to? It was all her fault; she could have chosen to stay in London, even to be taken into the workhouse.

Before long the frantic clattering, the heat of the room, weariness and worry overcame her. She couldn't keep her eyes open, couldn't stand upright;

she was hot and sick and dizzy. She slumped forward, heard a woman's shriek over the machinery rattle, and felt herself being wrenched backwards by two strong arms knotted round her waist. The machine had stopped. The overlooker was standing over her, his face nearly purple with rage. He was shouting at Moll because she had stopped the machine, and Moll was yelling back at him, "I 'ad to stop it or lass'd be dead."

"I'll dock you one hour's wages for this, Moll," he growled. "Both of you!" He started the machine back up and glared at them till they took up their work again.

At one o'clock, the apprentices were sent out to the yard for dinner, which was cold porridge. It was bitterly cold out there, especially after the heat of the spinning shed. Emily was too tired to talk, almost too tired to walk. All the children had wisps of cotton on their clothing, as if they had been caught in sleet. They clustered together for warmth, and when the food came most of them ate in complete silence, as weary as she was. Only Bess's voice could be heard, chattering to Lizzie, who was looking pale and exhausted and hardly answering except with nods and smiles. She kept looking round, and when she saw Emily she waved to her, relieved. Emily was almost too tired to wave back.

Sam crouched next to her, his porridge cupped in his hands like a ball of grey snow. "Rough lot, those overlookers, ain't they? I got Crick, and cor! His fist is like a coconut! I got my ear clipped from him, before I'd even done any work! And it stinks rotten in there. Worse than the closets, ain't it? You all right, Em'ly? You look ghosty white."

She smiled weakly at him. He was doing his best to be friendly, she knew, but she really wanted to escape into her own dark and lonely thoughts.

"'Ere, eat up," he told her. "It's really tasty, this roast beef!"

Too soon the bell on the roof of the mill clanged for work to start again. Emily saw that the other apprentices were wiping their mouths with the back of their hands, wiping their hands on their clothes, and scurrying back to work. They had learnt the routine in no time. "Come on," said Sam. "Bit less'n five more hours work, and we might get some apple dumplings for tea."

The fresh air had woken Emily up a bit; she felt

sharper and brighter, more able to concentrate, and at first the afternoon went faster than the morning had. But by the end of the day her hands were chapped and cut with the threads, and her back was aching. She walked many miles up and down the aisle, looking, looking, looking, never daring to lift her eyes from the threads, and when the bell rang at six o'clock she jumped, startled out of a trance. Moll just lifted her hand. The apprentices were going home, but she had three more hours of work to do. Emily wondered whether she lived over that steep black hill, and whether she had children at home, waiting to be fed.

It was full dark again outside. She fished a pair of clogs out of the heap by the door and trudged wearily back to the house with the other apprentices. The first one out of the door had been given a lantern to carry, and they followed the swinging light in utter, exhausted silence. Lizzie caught up with Emily and they squeezed each other's hand tight, too tired to speak.

Seven years, Emily thought. *Seven more years until we're free.*

*

It wasn't apple dumplings for tea, but porridge again, this time with a few lumps of vegetables floating in it, and served in a wooden bowl, which they had to dip into a barrel of oatmeal to clean. They sat with the other apprentices who had been at the mill for weeks or months now, and Emily noticed that every one of them ate as if the meal was a banquet. Most of them seemed to have bad coughs, and drank mug after mug of watery ale. Her throat was dry from the dust of the spinning shed, and sore from trying to shout back when Moll was talking to her. The older apprentices, she noticed, had the way of reading each others' lips, so they talked together in a mumbling, almost soundless way, exaggerating the vowel sounds by stretching their lips into wide, comical shapes. She saw Bess and Lizzie pulling faces and giggling together as they tried to carry on a conversation in the same way, till Mrs Cleggins hoisted Bess from her bench and led her to the front of the room.

"This lass has ever such a lot to say for herself," she announced. "I wonder if she can say her ABC?"

No. Bess couldn't.

"Then slide your bowls away all of you. Skivvy,

collect them all in. Give out slates and sand. And every one of you, write your ABC. If you can't, sit with someone who can, and learn it. And don't talk. We'll have an hour's schooling, while I go to my room for my tea. Then bed."

After an hour when they did nothing at all except yawn and draw stick figures and spidery shapes with their fingers, Mrs Cleggins returned, wiping her mouth with the back of her hand, sucking shreds of food from under her teeth, and the room fell silent. She made no attempt to check their work. The sand was shaken from the slates, the slates collected in, and the boys were ordered to go up to the top room and the girls to follow the housekeeper to their dormitory.

"Bed!" Emily sighed to Lizzie. "I can't wait! I could sleep on my feet."

"Like a horse!" Bess whispered, and she and Lizzie started giggling again. The dormitory was a long, bare room with beds with chamber pots underneath, and a row of cloaks on hooks. There was no fire in the room, and the windows rattled in the draught of rainy wind. Mrs Cleggins told them all to kneel down and say their prayers, and then to climb into bed, still wearing the work shifts that stank of grease. They all had cotton fluff in their hair. Emily and Lizzie snuggled up together, but when Mrs Cleggins walked down the rows of beds she pulled back the blanket, yanked Lizzie out of Emily's arms, and dragged her out of the bed.

"No, you will not sleep with your sister!" she muttered. "Sisters make trouble, always have done." She led her to another bed, pulled a strange girl out of it and made her swap places with Lizzie. "You go in with her sister," she told her.

A coughing, lanky girl with feet like lumps of ice climbed into Emily's tight bed. Then, without a word of goodnight, Mrs Cleggins left the dormitory, taking the candle and her hefty shadow with her. She locked the door behind her.

13

A PATTERN OF SUNDAYS

It seemed to Emily that she had only just closed her eyes when a fiercely jangled bell startled her out of her sleep.

"What's happening?" she asked, scared, not knowing for the moment where on earth she was.

"It's five o'clock bell," the girl sharing her bed told her. "Best get up sharp, or Mrs Cleggins'll beat you."

And so the second day of their lives at the mill began, and was little different from the first, except that Emily's overlooker watched her balancing on the tips of her toes to reach her threads and yanked her away from her machine. Without saying a word to her he pushed her down to the floor and shoved her under the machine, and she realised that she had lost her job as a piecer and had been turned into a scavenger, like her sister, and it was just as frightening, and just as bone-wearying, and the minutes, the hours, the days stretched until they seemed to last for ever, with only the comfort of a hard bed every night.

But on Sunday there was no work. After breakfast the baskets of clothes and boots were brought in. Lizzie danced with excitement at the thought of having her own dress back for the day, with Ma's patches on the elbows, and the piece of ribbon she had sewn on by herself to look like a butterfly. It was part of her past – the nearest thing to home. But she was given a pale, faded dress with big black buttons sewn up the back, and a hem that dipped as if a clog had been caught in it. She held it up to show Emily, bitterly disappointed.

"It's not my dress!" she said. "Mrs Cleggins, you've given me the wrong dress."

"I'll have none of your grumblings!" Mrs Cleggins snapped. She slapped Lizzie's face so hard that it left a red, hand-shaped mark on cheek. "Do you want to wear your work clothes to church? Like a pauper? Be thankful to have clothes to change into."

"This dress is too tight on me," Miriam muttered when Mrs Cleggins had moved on past. "I can hardly breathe in it!"

Robin smiled his dazzling smile at her. "You look very dainty," he told her, and she curtsyed to him, smiling back, with her white cheeks turning pink.

Mrs Cleggins snorted. "I'm watching! Get your cloaks, line up, and hurry to church."

The church was more than an hour's walk up over the steep hill and down the other side to the village of Oldcastle, where most of the mill workers lived. In places steps had been carved into the boulders to make the walking easier for the workers to come up and down every day. They were slippery after the night's rain, and Lizzie and Emily grabbed at one another from time to time, laughing with the effort of simply staying upright. They were giddy with happiness. It was wonderful to be out in the air, to be wearing clothes that didn't stink of work, to have a whole day of freedom in front of them. As they struggled up, panting, to the crest of the hill that lay between Bleakdale and Oldcastle, the bells of the village church rang out to greet them like a burst of birdsong. Bess spread out her arms so her cloak lifted up and out around her like the wings of a kestrel. "Watch me fly!" she shouted. "I'm on top of the world, I am!" Lizzie caught her hands and they whirled each other round, shouting with laughter. Emily watched them, biting her lip. A knot of loneliness clenched her stomach. Ma would be glad that Lizzie had found a friend. So should she be. She turned her back on them so she was looking down away from the shadowed slopes of Bleakdale towards the green valley of Oldcastle.

"It's not so bad, after all," she told herself. "At least I'll always be happy on Sundays. How many Sundays will there be in seven years? If there's four in a month, and sometimes five...and there's twelve months in a year..." and she spent the rest of the scramble down to the church trying to count all the Sundays she would have until she was free.

By the time they reached the church the mill owner's family had arrived. They had come by carriage, taking the long, bumpy valley cart track that would have been about seven miles to walk. Dulcie, the girl with cold feet who shared Emily's bed, told her who they all were, as one by one the Blackthorn family emerged from their carriage. They watched a grey-haired man being half carried out and placed in a wheelchair. Emily saw that his eyes were bright like a bird's, sharp to everything round him. He had tufts of white hair sprouting from his nostrils, as if he had been sniffing cotton fluff.

"That's Master Blackthorn, in the chair," Dulcie said, turning her head away. "Don't stare. He's a cripple. They say he broke his back years ago, when machinery was being put into the mill. There were riots, they say, and he was nearly killed by his own workers. That's why he always looks so angry at us, as if he hates us all. Some of the older women say he used to be a kind man, before his accident." She shuddered. "Not now though."

"I've seen that other man," Emily said. "The one in the yellow waistcoat. He came to look at us, first morning we came here."

"That's Master Blackthorn's son, Master Crispin. He might look like a daffodil, but he can bark at you like a dog when he has a mind. All he cares about is how much profit the mill makes in a day. And there's the daughter, Miss Sarah, and we all love her. When they do the hymns, listen out for her voice, because it's like honey, it's so sweet. And Mistress Blackthorn, her mother, she's as prickly as her name. She never comes into the mill – never. Never even looks at us. I don't think she knows we exist! We have to get into our benches quick because they like to make an entrance as if they was proper gentry. And remember, we mustn't stare at Master Blackthorn."

"I can't help it," Emily whispered. "I feel sorry for him. I think he looks sad, not angry."

"If he's sad, it's because he can't run the mill like he wants to. He has to leave it to Master Crispin, and *he* acts as if it all belongs to him already!"

After church came the long walk back to the apprentice house. Emily was still in high spirits from the walk, and the sound of the hymns and Miss Sarah's honey voice was still with her. She still hadn't worked out how many Sundays there would be in the seven years; they were spread out ahead of her like stars in the Milky Way. They were there to enjoy, not to count.

That day they had a special Sunday dinner of porridge with some grey lumps of meat in it and a few even greyer floating vegetables. Sam's cheeks bulged with pleasure at the sight of it. "Meat! Ain't this heaven!" he sighed.

"Heaven!" grumbled Miriam. "The meat's so tough I can't even chew it."

"Give it here then," Sam offered. "I'll chew it for you!"

"Get a move on!" Mrs Cleggins shouted. "Clear up fast, wipe grease off your desks. You can do your nattering later. It's school time now."

Emily smiled round at Lizzie, excited. Now, at last, she would learn to read and write. She would be able to do sums, she would learn about things she had never even seen. But although they were given slates, they were given no letters or numbers to copy. Mrs Cleggins walked round the room reciting Bible stories off by heart.

"Listen, and learn," she told them at the end of each story. "They stay in your head, and you never forget them."

Robin yawned loudly, bored, and was given a slash across his hand with the cane. Eventually Mrs Cleggins seemed to have run out of stories. She gave them each a scoop of sand, which they were to scatter across their slates. "Now you can draw pictures of your favourite Bible story," she said. "And that's your Sunday treat."

While they drew with their fingers on the sand she continued to pace round the room, slapping hands and pulling hair if she didn't like what she saw, caning anyone who giggled or spoke out of turn. From time to time she gazed out of one of the high windows as if she wanted to be free, like one of the black crows flapping into the trees. Then she would snap round again, looking for a hand to slap. And then suddenly, as if she was as bored as Robin, she told them to shake the sand off the slates into the bucket. School was over.

"Free time now," she said. "It's only time you'll get to yourselves in whole week. Make most of it."

"I hope Crick ain't out there, glaring at us all," Sam muttered. "I can't get 'im out of my 'ead, Em'ly. Even when I'm dreaming, 'e's still there, flicking his whip at me." He stood in the doorway, peering round the edge of the building, before he stepped outside.

Emily looked round for Lizzie, but she and Bess were already running out together, away from the dark cave of the schoolroom and into the pale sunlight of the end of the day.

So the procession of Sundays fell into a pattern. Gradually the light at the end of the day grew shorter. Soon it was almost dark by the time school was over, but no one wanted to stay in the dim schoolroom for the rest of their precious day off. The boys found dams to make and break in the stream, trees to climb, stones to skim. Robin organised competitions to see who could be fastest, strongest, bravest. He had a group of two or three workhouse boys who were always with him, always willing to do anything he told them. Miriam called them his gang of thugs, though she wouldn't have a word said against Robin. He was always the winner. The younger boys did their best to compete, always pressed by Robin to join in, but he led the jeers when they failed miserably and fell out of the trees or into the stream. Emily hated Robin for that, especially when he taunted Sam, who didn't have a head for heights at all.

"You're worse than a girl, Sam Jenkins!" Robin teased. "Come on, Miriam, show him how to do it! Jump over the stream!"

"No, I'll get the hang of it! That's how you get good at fings!" Sam muttered. "You just do it again and again. Like this!"

"Win, Sam! Win!" Emily found herself shouting

when Robin was urging all the boys on to see who could jump the furthest across the stream. To everyone's surprise, Sam did win. He grinned as though he was king of the world.

"I would have done it!" Miriam shouted. "Ask me again next time."

Robin smiled at Miriam then, and she tittered to Emily behind her hand. "He reminds me of my brother," she said. "He's full of dash, isn't he?"

"I didn't know you had a brother," said Emily, surprised.

"Well, I don't any more," Miriam said. "Gone for ever, he is."

Emily bit her lip, remembering Jim: happy, skipping Jim. Where was he now? she wondered. *Oh, be safe, little Jim. Be well. Somewhere.*

One Sunday, Sam found a length of rope and Robin organised everyone into teams to play tug-o'war with it. Everyone seemed to want to be in Robin's team, except Emily. But Miriam dragged her in.

"We'll have boys against girls," she said. "I reckon I'm as strong as any lad here."

So they all joined in, screaming and laughing, till

Mrs Cleggins shouted through the window that they were giving her a headache, and the teams collapsed into shrieking piles on top of one another.

"My hands are buzzing!" Lizzie laughed. She danced up to Emily to show the scarlet palms of her hands, already blistering "That's the best fun I've ever had!"

Sometimes on fine days Mrs Cleggins brought a chair outside and sat half dozing, immediately alert if anyone wandered off out of sight. The boys hung about in groups then, lounging and joking. The girls strolled up and down the tracks, arm in arm, whispering secrets. Lizzie and Bess were inseparable now. Sometimes it hurt Emily to see how close they were.

She noticed one Sunday that they were gathering twigs and wild flowers and running off down towards the river with them.

"What are you doing?" she called after them.

"Making a den," Lizzie called back.

"Can I help?" she asked, but it seemed that they didn't hear her. She turned away, and saw Dulcie and Miriam standing watching, waiting for her to join them. She didn't feel she wanted their prattle, their coarse laughter, their endless talk about boys. She just lifted her hand to them, and pretended to search for flowers to give to Lizzie for the den. That was when she saw something white gleaming in the shrubbery. She knelt down to see it properly. It was the skeleton of an animal. She prised it out onto the path, and turned it over gently with the end of a stick, a bit timid about touching a dead thing with her hands. The skull peered up at her with its sightless eye sockets. Its tiny teeth were intact.

"It's a hare, that is."

She looked round, and saw that Sam had crouched down next to her.

"How do you know?"

"I just know. I always know these things," he said. "Look at its legs, how long they are! See how it stretches out, how it all joins up! You can tell how they can spring when they run. You seen 'em run, ain't you, pounding up the hills as if the whole world was after them. Hares is witches really, some people say."

She laughed up at him. "Sam! You don't really believe that, do you?"

He shrugged, shy. "I don't know, do I? I don't

know if what people says is true or not."

"What are you looking at?" Lizzie and Bess ran up to them, panting, and crouched down beside them.

"It's a hare," Emily explained. "Sam says they're witches." She looked round, but Sam had slipped away, back to join Robin and the older boys she supposed. "You could have it for your den."

"Ooh. A dead thing?" Bess said, doubtful. "We just want pretty things, don't we, Lizzie?"

"I think it would be nice," Emily said. "Special."

She stood up again. She had liked that moment with Sam. That was a special thing too, to store in the den of her mind. She walked away from Lizzie and Bess, and when she came back down the path later with Miriam and Dulcie, the hare had gone.

She didn't mention it to them. She knew they wouldn't understand. They'd shriek and shudder at the thought of touching it and examining it.

"Let's go and watch the boys," Miriam suggested, but Emily knew that it was Robin they really wanted to see. He stood in the centre of the circle, and the other boys jostled round him, laughing at his jokes.

"Isn't he good-looking!" Dulcie whispered.

"Is he?" Emily said. "I hadn't noticed."

"Go on!" Dulcie laughed. "I saw you watching him!"

But Emily wasn't watching Robin. She didn't like him; she didn't like the way the other boys hung round him like flies, as if they had no minds of their own. It seemed to Emily that they would do anything he told them to. She was watching Sam. He was so simple and happy; he didn't have the roughness of the other boys, or the confidence of Robin. She remembered what he had told her once about working with his dad in the stables. She could imagine that. She could picture him being careful and thorough, brushing the horses down till their coats were smooth and glossy, listening to them and minding them.

"Remind you of a boy back home, does he?" Dulcie teased.

Emily shook her head. "I didn't know any boys," she said. "Only Jim."

And there it came again, that yearning moment from the past. Again she had a sharp memory of Jim skipping into their tenement room, clutching the steaming pie in his hands, flushed and happy with running, full of pride because he'd done what Ma had told him to do. She remembered the pie, oozing with gravy and rich with good meat, and how Ma had turned her face away from it, too ill to eat. Jim had paused, puzzled, understanding at last, perhaps, how ill Ma was, and then, to please her, he had finished up every bit of the pie.

"Jim?" Miriam asked.

"My little brother. But I'll never see him again."

14

WINTER

Before long, the deep winter came. They walked to work in the ice, their breath smoking away from them, their hands blue with cold. Snow piled in deep drifts up the hillside; no workers threaded their way from Oldcastle. Eventually, the river froze, and the wheel refused to turn. The machines stood idle, like the skeletons of ancient beasts. The trees were silent ghosts: the river, the wild creatures, the birds; all silent as death – waiting. The apprentices were shooed out of the house by Mrs Cleggins.

"You still have to work!" she told them. "Can't lounge round here all day. Still have to earn your keep!"

"What can we do though?" Sam asked. "The mill's shut, isn't it?"

Mrs Cleggins shut the door smartly in his face.

"We can slide!" Robin said. He clambered carefully up a slippery bank of sheer ice. "Watch me!" He set off at a run, and slid gracefully down the slope, arms spread out each side of him like a bird. "Who can do it without falling over, eh?"

One by one the children followed him, shrieking and slipping, clutching one another and howling with laughter. They could see Mrs Cleggins watching them from the window of the apprentice house, and they didn't care. There was no work to do while the mill was closed.

Suddenly Mrs Cleggins rapped sharply on the window, waving her arms at them to stop. "Ignore her!" Robin ordered. "Keep on playing!" But she pulled open the door, and her face was scarlet as she stood there with her arms folded.

"What are you doing?" she shouted, as if she'd only just noticed them and their noise. "Get off to mill. There's no time for playing."

It was Emily who realised that she was looking beyond them at the track that led to the mill owner's house. She turned and saw Master Crispin approaching them, swinging his walking cane, his face grim with anger.

"Playing, sliding, laughing, on a work day?" he shouted, and his furious voice rose and echoed, and silence fell. The apprentices stood as if ice had turned them to statues, and their breath choked back laughter and danced about them like white smoke.

"But the mill ain't working, Master Crispin," said Bess bravely. She waved her hand towards the silent mill building. "What's there to do, please?"

"What's there to do? Clean the machines, and clean 'em again!" he barked. "Clean 'em every day till the thaw comes."

In single file the apprentices made their way silently up to the mill, darting amused and puzzled glances at one another. Master Crispin followed them and watched till every child was stationed at a machine. Then he sent Bess down to the lower floor.

"You can dole out the cleaning cloths and brooms," he told her. "And don't dally. There's been enough time wasted already."

And like a black ghost Crick appeared, whip tucked under his arm, scowling resentfully at every child as he passed them by. When Sam stood up to stretch himself, Crick gave him a push that sent him sprawling onto the floor. "Who told you to stand up?" he snarled. His stick thwacked across Sam's back. "Stay on floor, where you belong."

Later in the day Master Blackthorn was carried

up the lane in his wheelchair by his servant Fergus, and wheeled up and down the long, silent aisles of still machinery. He nodded at the apprentices while they worked.

"I like to see my mill sparkling clean," he said. "These are beautiful machines, eh, Crispin? Proud of them, aren't I? Bleakdale Mill, the cleanest in the country! Thanks to these young people here."

Master Crispin stood silent, glaring around him in anger.

"He thinks he owns it," Miriam mouthed at Emily, only this time it wasn't because the clatter of machinery would drown her voice. "Thinks he owns us, too. Only he don't. He don't care about us like Master Blackthorn does."

Master Crispin strode up to her and hissed down at her. "No slacking! Every minute you waste loses us money." And as he passed Emily straightened up and pulled a face at his back, just like all the workers did.

It was a relief to everyone when the thaw came. The wheel tugged its way round, groaning through the slabs of ice, then rode freely again. The machines clattered to life, the workers returned, Master Crispin rubbed his hands with pleasure. Now the snow was inside again instead of outside: the snow of the drifting cotton. It clung to their hair, their clothes, they breathed in the fibres. At night in the dormitory the girls gasped and coughed and wheezed, hung onto the pockets of air at the top of their lungs. They felt as if they were drowning in fibre dust.

And then into that lonely darkness there gradually came the scuttling of mice, the sighing of wood shifting against wood, the shivering call of owls and, far away, the wail of crying children.

"What's that?" Emily sat up in bed sharply.

"'Tis Mistress Blackthorn, turned into a ghost!" Dulcie said. "I dream about her every night, with her eyes all blank and scary, tiptoeing about the way she goes up the aisle in the church."

"'Tis the wind, bless you," muttered one of the older apprentices. "Get your head down and sleep, Emily. You need rest, you do."

"'Tis never the wind, and you know that well, May," came another voice. "'Tis the dead 'prentice children in the graveyard."

"It must be a lonely place to be, out there on the hillside," another girl said. "And no gravestone even to say who they are. They're lost children, ain't they? No one will ever know they're there. They're lost and lonely, and that's why they cry, every now and then. It's not a proper burial ground. It's too hard for them to bear."

"Will you stop it?" May snapped. "I shall never get to sleep now. It's the wind, I tell you. The wind in the trees, that's all."

"Why did they die?" That was Bess, in a tiny, trembling voice.

"Cholera."

"Plague."

"This awful cough we all get with the cotton dust."

"Caught in machines."

The voices came out of the darkness, as if the dead children themselves were telling their tales. There was a sudden loud thumping on the floor and they all started with fright and fear. "I can hear you!" came Mrs Cleggins's voice from her room below. "I'll have not a sound more, or every one of you will be standing out in yard all night."

They lay in scared silence, till Bess's voice came again. "I hope I never go there. Please, please, don't let anyone put me in the lost children's graveyard."

15

MISS BLACKTHORN

Only Sunday made the working week worth living through. It was like the glimmer of sunlight on the edge of a brooding cloud. All through the aching and bending and scavenging, the endless rumble and clatter of machinery, Emily and Lizzie held the thought of Sunday in their minds. As the days began to lengthen they had longer to stay out in the air after school time, warming themselves in the spring sunshine before the shadow of the hillside ate it up. Even Mrs Cleggins responded to the sun; she sat on a fallen log and held her face up to it, like a daisy.

One Sunday Mrs Cleggins was called away after church to visit her sick father. Skivvy was smug with pride at being left in sole charge. She gaped around at the apprentices, beaming her toothless grin as if it was a special treat for them to have their gruel without Mrs Cleggins looking on.

"A bit of extra meat, Skivvy?" Sam asked. "It's

so delicious. I could eat meat all day, I could."

"There's no more meat," Robin said, peering into Skivvy's cauldron. "I bet Mrs Cleggins told Skivvy to cook less today, as she's away. You can have more porridge though. Plenty of that." He dolloped another grey, slimy pile into his bowl. "I like to see boys eating," he added, in Mrs Cleggins's voice.

Skivvy grinned, enjoying the fun. She finished off the rest of the gruel herself, licking the ladle and sighing with pleasure. "What a feast!"

"Now what do we do?" Robin asked. "Have we got the whole afternoon off?"

"School, as usual," Skivvy told him. "That's what Mrs Cleggins said."

"We don't even have slates to draw on," Bess said. "She keeps 'em locked in her room. I like drawing."

They stared at Skivvy and she rubbed her elbows uselessly, all her smugness gone. "I don't know what to teach you," she said at last. "I don't know anything."

"I'll teach them," Robin said. He jumped up from his bench and strode to the front of the classroom. "You go and cook us something nice for tea, Skivvy."

He lifted the cane from its hook on the wall and

paced round the room, whipping the air with it. "Don't slouch. Sit up straight. Arms folded on desk. Don't twiddle. And you can just swallow that grin o' yours, Samuel Jenkins, or you'll be grinning on other side o' your head." He could do her voice exactly, even the flat vowel sounds she made, and the way she made the word "the" disappear from everything she said, and the clacking of her teeth when she was annoyed.

Lizzie starting giggling, and he strode up to her and swished the cane across her desk, making her jump. The girl sitting in front of her got a slap on the cheek, which made her cry.

"What did you do that for?" she asked.

"That's just in case you was thinking of laughing!" he told her. "First lesson in this school is be'ave. Say it!"

At first it was funny, but he was too good at cuffing and slapping, and he improvised little sharp kicks at shins by turning his clog neatly sideways as he walked past the rows of tables. "Stop mithering me," he snapped at them. *Clack clack clack* went his teeth, *crack* went his cane across exposed hands. The children in the middle of the rows were safe;

135

they couldn't stop laughing and muttering taunting remarks at him.

"I wish you'd stop it, Robin Small," Bess stood up and shouted at him at last. "You're just a silly show-off, you."

"Come here and be caned!" he shouted at her. "I'll have no cheek from you."

The whole class had erupted into the chaos of laughter and shouting when the door opened and Miss Sarah Blackthorn walked in, carrying a large basket. The apprentices fell into complete silence.

"Good afternoon, children," Miss Sarah said. Her voice was trembling slightly, as if perhaps she was nervous. "I heard Mrs Cleggins is away for the rest of the day, and I thought I'd pretend to be your teacher for a bit and do some writing with you. Would you like that?"

There was a hum of happiness, like bees in a flowerbed. One of the boys gave a little cheer, and wasn't told off for it.

Miss Sarah floated down the aisles giving out pieces of paper that had been cut into small squares.

"What will we do with this, Miss Sarah?" Sam asked.

"Why, you'll write on it!" she said, smiling. "But first, you have to make ink to write with. Perhaps one of you boys would be kind enough to scrape a little soot from the back of the fireplace for me?"

She held up a wooden bowl, and there was a rapid scuffling of feet as boys elbowed each other out of the way in the rush to get to the fireplace first. The winning boy, Alfie, dived into the fireplace as if he was wanting to be a little chimney sweep and climb right up inside it, but eventually he emerged triumphant, soot in his hair and his cheeks and all over his hands, and presented the bowlful to Miss Sarah. She sent him outside to wash himself down and to bring back a jug of water.

"Now," she said. "I'm going to start by showing you all how to make ink with soot and water, then I'm going to let each of you make some for yourselves. And I'll give you all quills to write with. Have you ever written with quills?"

She took a sprig of white goose feathers from her basket and held it up in the air.

The apprentice children all shook their heads, mystified. They had only ever written with their fingers before, tracing shapes into the sand Mrs

Cleggins scattered onto their slates. Even in the workhouse classroom they had never been given quills.

"Well, we have a lot of lovely things to learn!" Miss Sarah said. "After you've made your ink, I'll show you how to sharpen your quills, and then we'll be ready to write. A little soot in the pot, a little water. Stir it round." They watched her, fascinated. "Everyone have a go at that, just come out to the front, don't be scared. Watch me, and copy what I do."

The children soon had ink all over their faces and hands, but Miss Blackthorn didn't seem to mind at all. She told them to carry their little pots of ink carefully to their desks, and then she went to every child in turn and showed them how to make curvy shapes by dipping the goose feathers into the ink and scratching them across the paper.

"Miss, my shapes look like dead flies!" one girl giggled.

"Mine look like snail trails!" another one said, and there were bursts of laughter around the room; quick spontaneous flares that were smothered instantly, anxious glances darted at Miss Sarah. But she just smiled and nodded and carried on quietly moving around the room, sometimes stooping to guide a fisted hand to make the right shape.

"You're doing really well!" she said, clapping her hands. "I'm going to write some letters on the board now, and I want you to copy them as carefully as you can. Don't worry if you get them wrong. I'll help you."

She turned away to the board, and Emily risked a glance round the classroom. Some of the apprentices were biting their lips with concentration, bent over their little pieces of paper and breathing slowly and carefully as if their work might disappear at any moment. Some, like Sam, were just grinning broadly with sheer pleasure.

"Of all the Sundays we've had," Emily whispered to Lizzie, "this one is the best yet."

Lizzie nodded. "And lessons are usually the part I hate. I didn't know school could be like this. I'd like to have lessons every day, now. Just school, and no scavenging!"

"There, that's all the letters of the alphabet." Miss Sarah turned round from the board, dusting the chalk from her hands so it clouded down her dress. She laughed and wiped the dust away. "When you know those, you can read and write everything. It will open the whole world for you." She frowned slightly then, as if she had only just remembered that these were mill children she was talking to. "If you know the letters already, you could write your own names," she added, flustered. "I really don't know what stage you're at. And don't worry about getting anything wrong. I'm only a pretend teacher, remember."

She wandered round the room, showing them how to hold their goose quills, laughing at the ink smudges they made on the paper, guiding the hands of the lucky ones to make clear, recognisable shapes of letters, praising the ones who managed their copying on their own.

"Miss Blackthorn, why can't you come every Sunday?" Sam asked, and Bess clapped. "That's what I was going to say!"

"I only came today because Mrs Cleggins is visiting her father," Miss Blackthorn said, smiling. "But I'm sure you enjoy lessons with her."

"No, we don't," one of the older boys said. "She can't even spell her own name, never mind ours."

"And she hits us all the time," someone else muttered. "We hate her."

Miss Sarah looked at the boy in horrified silence. "She *hits* you?"

"All the time. She beats us with that stick on the wall."

Miss Sarah put her hand to her mouth, then turned away. She picked up her gloves and her bag and hurried out of the schoolroom.

The door swung to and fro, to and fro, groaning.

16

I KNEW YOUR MA

The children sat in silence, waiting for her to come back in, though they knew she wouldn't. The spell had been broken; they were back in the cold sunlight of late afternoon, with nothing left to do except wait for their work to start again. In silence Emily stood up to gather up the pieces of paper. Lizzie followed her, collecting the feather quills, carefully carrying the pots of ink to the teacher's table. They would have to be cleaned and put away somewhere before Mrs Cleggins came back. The other apprentices watched them in horrified silence, willing them to stop in case Miss Sarah came back in to start the lesson again.

"She looked as if she was going to cry," Miriam said at last.

"She's so kind and nice," Emily said when she came back to her place. "She made me think of my ma a bit, only she's younger."

"Did she?" Miriam said. "I never knew my ma."

"I think about her all the time. Her and Jim. I never stop thinking about them. I never will. I just wish I knew what's happened to them."

Robin stood up abruptly and opened the door. "I'm going out," he said. "Don't just sit there. Come outside. If you dare." He grinned round at them and every boy in the room stood up to follow him. He nodded, pleased with himself, and ran whooping up the track. One by one the girls drifted out too. Sam lingered by the door, hands in his pockets, as if he was waiting for someone.

"Thinks he's the boss, that Robin Small," Bess grumbled. "He was like that in the workhouse, wasn't he, Sam? Always wanting to be the boss. Always wanting everyone to do what he does. And they do."

"He's right though," said Sam. "Why sit in the schoolroom when there's no teacher, and it's sunny outside?" He looked wistfully after Robin and the younger boys, who were swarming up trees after him. "They're having a nice time."

"Why don't you join them?" Bess asked him. "I've a good mind to go climbing trees myself. Looks fun, that does."

"I will, in a minute. I just want "– he looked at Emily – "I just want to tell you something, Em'ly. On your own."

Emily blushed and Lizzie giggled.

"Go on." Bess gave Emily a little push.

"We can just go to our den for a bit, till Skivvy rings the bell for tea. Don't want to miss that, do we? Not Sunday tea," said Lizzie, and she and Bess scampered off.

Sam moved away, his head down, his hands still dug deep into his pockets.

"What did you want to tell me, Sam?" Emily called. "I don't want to miss my tea either."

He took off his cap and twisted it anxiously in his hands. "It's just that I think I know something that you ought to know, but I don't know how to say it. But I'm your friend, ain't I? I want to be your friend, Em'ly."

"Then tell me," she said. "But it's not something good, is it? I can tell by your face."

"No, it ain't," he agreed. He sank down onto a fallen tree trunk and she stood watching him nervously plucking at his cap.

"Go on."

"It's about your ma."

Her heart lurched. "Ma?"

"I heard you talking about her just now, and I thought, go on, Sam, go on, do it."

She said nothing, but bit her lip, watching him.

Sam sighed. "Well, that day when I first saw you outside the workhouse, Lizzie was asking a boy called Tip about your ma and your brother, and he said they weren't there." He wiped his hand across his eyes. "But I fink he might have been wrong, Em'ly. Cos the night before, a boy *had* come in with his mother."

"Was he called Jim?"

"I don't know his name. But the mother was very sick, like Lizzie said, and Mr Sissons don't like sick people being brought in because they might have cholera and spread it, and they can't work or nuffin'. Me and an old man called Joseph had to take this sick lady straight up to the infirmary, and Joseph asked me to sit with her for a bit because he didn't know where her boy was. She looked a lot like you, Em'ly. She was whispering names, and it was hard to hear what she said, but it was three names. I know what they are now."

"Emily, Lizzie, Jim," Emily said slowly, flatly.

"That was it." Sam put his cap on and then took it off again and twisted it round and round in his hands. "So I fink I knew your ma."

Emily sat down next to him then. She stared steadily at the ground, where a blackbird was busily scrabbling among grasses for twigs and leaves to make a nest with.

"What happened to her?"

"She went to sleep," Sam said "But she never woke up, Em'ly. She died that night."

Mrs Cleggins returned after tea that day. She told the apprentices that she'd had a long, weary day and needed an early night, so they must all go to bed too, even though it was scarcely dark outside yet.

Emily and Lizzie didn't care. They had sat in lonely silence through the meal, eating nothing, silently wiping away the tears that coursed down their cheeks. *Poor Jim*, Emily kept thinking. *He's all on his own now. At least we've got each other, me and Lizzie.*

Sam watched them, as distressed as they were. *I*

wish I hadn't told her now, he thought. *I've made them sad, that's what I've done. But if it was my ma, I'd want to know.*

The girls trudged upstairs after the meal, and when they knelt down together for prayers, Lizzie rested her head on Emily's shoulder. There were no prayers in her mind. She could only think one thing: *Ma's dead, I know that now. I'll never see her again.* When she opened her eyes she saw that Mrs Cleggins was sitting on one of the beds, watching them.

"What's going on?" the woman asked.

"We've heard that our mother has died," Emily whispered. Beside her, Lizzie sobbed again. Emily put her arm round her. "One of the boys told me. He was in the workhouse hospital with her."

Mrs Cleggins stood up. They thought she was going to shout at them or slap them, but instead she simply said, "You can sleep in same bed tonight."

She continued her rounds, lighting her way with her candle, and then left. A time of quiet hushed the room as each girl fell into her own darkness, her own quiet misery. Emily stroked Lizzie's hair until she felt her slipping at last into sleep.

"That's it," Emily whispered. "You sleep, and have nice dreams of before we came here. We got to look after each other, Lizzie. We got to stay close. We're orphans now."

17

CRUEL CRICK

Getting up in the mornings was harder than ever. Somehow Lizzie and Emily got through the next days and weeks, comforting each other, letting the trance of work ease away their grief.

"There's not a soul here who hasn't lost someone," Miriam told them. "Most of us haven't got anyone at all. And if we have, we're never going to see them again, stuck here. Stuck here for ever."

They had been at the mill for months, and they knew the routine of work as if they had never had any other life. They had all learnt to lip-read by now, and at least it helped with the boredom of work. Whenever they dared to lift their eyes from the chirring machinery and spinning threads, they stole the chance to mouth something to someone; it was the only thing they could do to make themselves feel like human beings rather than bits of machinery. They had a little chant that they would mouth to one another, and each one would add something to the litany. "Food stinks," one of them would mouth, and the next one would turn towards another apprentice; "Food stinks, bed hurts," "Food stinks, bed hurts, work breaks me back," "Food stinks, bed hurts, work breaks me back, feet ache," and so on, and the game was to repeat it all without forgetting any words, and they had to be in the right order, before you added your complaint to the list. It made them laugh out loud sometimes. One time, Emily was waiting for Sam on the next machine to look round in her direction so she could mouth the list to him, and Crick pounced on her from behind. He was like a spider, winding his way around the clattering machines, his willow whip held firm under his arm. He put his hand under her chin and twisted her face round.

"Standing still. Looking where you shouldn't be. Laughing!" His face loomed over her, his mouth opening and shutting so close to hers that she could smell his breath, could taste his spittle. He raised his whip to lash her and Sam left his machine and pounced on Crick, tugging his arm away from Emily, trying to wrench the whip out of his hand. With a roar of rage that could be heard above the din Crick turned his whip on Sam, beating him again and again till Sam writhed on the floor in agony. Moll, Emily's spinner, shrieked for help as she tried to pull Emily away from the rolling bodies on the floor. The other workers watched in mute horror, and suddenly another man was there: Master Crispin the mill owner's son. He pulled Crick away from Sam and forced him to drop the whip. Crick stood back, panting, saliva dripping from his mouth like a mad dog. Sam crawled away on his hands and knees.

"Get outside!" Master Crispin shouted. "You deserve a whipping, both of you! And you, workers, stop gawping, stop wasting time. Time is money!"

He jerked his head for Sam and Crick to follow him outside. Emily stepped over to help Sam, but he shook his head and limped after the two other men.

Aghast at what they had seen, the apprentices worked on, heads down, eyes fastened on their work. They didn't look at one another. Emily was trembling. *Poor Sam, poor Sam*, she kept thinking. *It was all my fault.*

Eventually Crick came back in, snarling, eyes screwed up with hatred. He came up to Emily and grasped her arm so tightly that it hurt.

"You get no dinner today," he growled in her ear. He carried on down the lines of machines, grasping each one of the apprentices in turn, shaking the ones who seemed to protest. When dinnertime came and the workers went out to get their gruel, all the apprentices stayed on to clean the machines and the floors, while Crick prowled among them, gloating. Master Blackthorn was wheeled into the building by his servant.

"Let me see 'em. Roll me down, Fergus, so I can see 'em working."

Emily could hear the wheels creaking towards her, the slow wheezy rumbling of Master Blackthorn's breath as his chair rolled past her. "Work, work, work," he muttered. "Keep at it. That's it. Keep at it."

She daren't look up till he had passed, and then she gave herself a moment to stretch and ease the ache in her back. Robin caught Emily's eye.

"He'll pay for this," he mouthed. She shuddered. Did he mean Crick, she wondered. Or did he mean Sam?

She didn't see Sam again until teatime. He limped

into the apprentice house, and sat down carefully on the bench as if every bit of him was sore.

"What did Master Crispin say?" Emily asked, when she had a chance to go over to him.

"He barked at us both like a mad dog, worse than anyfin' I've ever heard. Made me shiver inside, worse than any beating. Then he told Crick he had to watch his temper or he'd swing for murder one day. And he told me I deserved a good crack, but he'd let me off this time, and I had to go and get cleaned up. Cor, Mrs Cleggins covered me in some smelly ointment what stung like I was in a nest of bees. Then I had to go back to work, and Master Crispin put me on another job, not on Crick's floor, and it's just as lovely up there because the overlooker has got a nice smiling face like a scorched cat."

"And we were all punished, just because you hit Crick to save your friend. Did you know that?" said Robin. "We worked all day long without our dinner. Do you think that's fair?"

Emily ignored him. "Thank you, Sam," she said quietly. He winced as she put her hand on his shoulder.

"Ow! It was nuffin'," he said.

"You should have grabbed the whip and let him taste it," Robin said. He smiled. "We will have our revenge, Sam, you and me. We will have our revenge on all of them."

18

SUNSHINE

The next Sunday was bright, with primroses under the walls and hedges, and the air was full of birdsong. Lizzie caught up with Emily as she made her way back from church, still singing one of the hymns under her breath.

"Winter's over, Lizzie! Things can only get better now," Emily told her. She squeezed her sister's hand and started singing again, and Lizzie joined in. Bess sprang up from behind them, showering them both with fuzzy catkins. She ran on, squealing with laughter, and Lizzie broke away from Emily and ran after her. Emily shrugged, disappointed that the moment of closeness was gone.

"Sunday is still my favourite day," she muttered. She turned round to Dulcie and Miriam. "Isn't it perfect!" she said.

"Aye, if we didn't have to spend the afternoon with Clackerty Cleggins, it would be!" Dulcie said.

"ABC. That's all I know!" Miriam said. "I remember what Miss Sarah showed me though. M for my name. I'm sure there's letters after that, but Cleggie has never told me 'em."

"Don't think about school. Think about the sunshine, and the birds, and look – the lambs in that far field!" Emily said. "Nothing could be better than that!"

But even school was wonderful that day. They were all sitting at their desks, hopelessly trying to copy the random and misshapen numbers that Mrs Cleggins had scrawled on the board, when the door was pushed open and in walked Miss Sarah and Master Crispin, still wearing his daffodil-coloured waistcoat under his jacket. But really, Emily thought, it was the only cheerful thing about him. He leant against the wall, staring round at the children with his sharp, shrewish eyes. Wherever he looked, the apprentices dropped their gaze, frightened in case he could read their thoughts. If he caught anyone's glance his eyes would glint, his face tighten, his whole body tense as if he was about to pounce. The only one in the room who didn't look away was Robin Small. He returned Master Crispin's stare, a slow smile playing across his face, as if they were equals. In the end it was Master Crispin who turned his head away.

But though they avoided Master Crispin's glare, every one of the children gazed at Miss Sarah, willing her to smile back at them. She walked down the rows between the long desks, asking this child their name, telling another that her eyes were a very pretty colour, praising another for his careful copying on the slate, and frowning if someone coughed.

"It's cotton dust, that awful cotton dust," she murmured. "You must breathe as much fresh air as you can, all of you. You must drink lots and lots of ale and water."

As she passed Lizzie she touched her lightly on the head. "Oh, if I had hair like yours!" she laughed, and went on her way, leaving Lizzie burning with pride.

"I got the same colour hair as Ma, ain't I, Emily?" she whispered.

"Like autumn leaves," Emily agreed. "That's what Pa used to say." And she looked away quickly, because Pa had died of cholera long ago, and now Ma was dead too, and their lives had changed for ever.

"Quiet!" Mrs Cleggins snapped. "Pay attention. Miss Sarah has something to say to you all."

Miss Sarah had come back to the front of the room. Her brother slid down onto a stool, his arms folded. He nodded at her to get on with it.

"Next Saturday is my birthday," Miss Sarah said. "And I want to give all you apprentices a present. It will be Buxford Fair on that day. My father has agreed to let you all have the day off to go to it."

There was a rustle of excitement, shouts of "Thank you, miss!"

Master Crispin stood up abruptly. "You must behave yourselves when you're there. You must act like young gentlemen and young ladies, not like the country ruffians who go to these places. And if anyone thinks of trying to run away, forget it! I have my stick, and I'll use it, you'll see."

His sister turned to him, still smiling. "Crispin, nobody would think of running away, I'm sure."

"Your overlookers will be there, keeping an eye on you." He glared round at them, and rested his gaze on Sam. "Mister Crick and Mister Grimshaw. They'll be there, be sure of that. You belong to us, remember? You belong to Bleakdale Mill."

There was a fizz of excitement when Miss Sarah and Master Crispin left. Even though Mrs Cleggins frowned and coughed and clapped her hands, she couldn't suppress it, couldn't get them to settle down again.

"Oh, get outside with you," she said at last. "Do as Miss Sarah said, and breathe some fresh air."

Robin was the first to move, as usual. He beckoned to Sam to join him. "I have a plan!" he called. "It'll just suit you."

Sam grinned round at Emily, proud to be singled out by Robin. Lizzie tried to tug Emily along to her favourite place by the river, where she and Bess had been making their den of branches.

"Aw, come with us!" Lizzie begged. "We've been working on it for ages, and it's nearly ready! I really want you to see it, Emily."

Emily hesitated. She looked over to where Sam was listening wide-eyed to Robin. She had only to sidle along the bushes to overhear what they were saying without being seen. And she looked at Lizzie, wide-eyed, happy Lizzie, begging her for once to join her and Bess.

"I want you to be the first to see it," Lizzie

pleaded. "Please, please, Emily."

"Right!" Emily said. "Show me."

But she kept glancing over her shoulder, wishing she could stay close to Sam. Whatever it was that Robin had to say to Sam would bring trouble, she was quite sure of that. She followed Lizzie and Bess down towards the river, scrambling this way and that under overgrown snagging bushes, crouching under an overhanging tree.

"You have to crawl for a bit here," Lizzie said. "It's the secret entrance, and no one else knows about it except you."

"Close your eyes," said Bess. Her voice was bubbling with excitement. "You'll be able to stand up in a minute, and you'll be inside the most beautiful place in the world. Like a palace, it is, only I'm not sure what a palace is, really! There, now."

"Welcome to our palace!" Lizzie chanted with her. They had been practising it, waiting for this special moment.

"Ain't this just the best thing you've ever seen?" Bess added, triumphant.

Emily gazed around, suddenly as excited as they were. They had made a house by weaving twigs and branches together, and they had decorated it with scraps of paper the children had used for their writing with Miss Sarah, threaded onto bits of cotton and slung across from one side to the other. There were still smudges of ink and spidery scrawls of writing on them. There were a couple of small logs for seats, and the floor was strewn with goose feathers. Tucked under a cascade of wild flowers was the hare skeleton, its bony skull grinning up at Emily.

"We come here and think happy thoughts, don't we, Bess?" Lizzie sat on one of the logs, hugging her knees. "We can forget about the machines and Master Crick and all that when we're in here."

"We just listen to the birds and think happy thoughts," said Bess. "And p'raps it's a bit like heaven. That's what it is. Heaven."

19

I CAN BUY OUR FREEDOM

It was two days before Emily knew anything about what Sam and Robin were planning. Sam dodged alongside her as she was hurrying along to work one morning, and tugged her elbow. "Em'ly," he said, in an urgent whisper. "Have you got any money?"

"Money?" she repeated, surprised. "What kind of money?"

"You know. Wages money. What other kind of money is there?"

"Why?"

"Because..." He stopped, and swung himself in front of her. "Because I can buy our freedom!" His eyes were shining. He was nearly choking with excitement.

"What are you talking about?"

"Robin is arranging for me to go back to London!"

"London! Don't be mad, Sam. He's having you on."

"He ain't! It's true! He wants to help me to get away from Crick."

"Crick?"

"You've seen how he has it in for me, haven't you? Always watching me, waiting to catch me out. He's a great black shadder following me everywhere. Robin says Crick will always have it in for me now, and I know he's right. He says I've got to get away from here. It's the only way. He said he could fix it for me, but I have to give him the money tonight."

Emily stopped. The other workers rushed on past her, elbowing her out of the way in their eagerness to get to work on time so as not to have their pay docked.

"I don't want to go without you, Em'ly," Sam said. "You're my friend. But I have to get away. I might never get another chance like this."

"Sam? Are you crazy? Come on, we're going to be late."

She started to walk on again, but he grabbed her arm. "Robin's arranging it all. One of the weavers knows there's a coach going from Buxford to London on Saturday! The day of the fair! I can have a cheap lift with them – all the way! I'd be free! Only I have to pay Robin tonight. And Em'ly, I've just thought – come with me! Say you will!"

Emily felt her heart lifting. London! She'd be going home. She could leave this dark, damp valley behind for ever. She'd find Jim, she'd find Rosie. Everything would be all right again, surely, if she could go back to London. "What about Lizzie?"

Sam shook his head. "There's only really room for one, Robin said. But you're scraggy thin, and so am I, so we could squeeze up and just take the place of one person, couldn't we? But not Lizzie as well. Besides, it'll take all the money I've got, and everything you could pay, just for me, really. But if you say you'll come I'll find a way for you to go too. I've just got to get some money. Robin says I can do jobs for him 'cos he's been so kind to me. I can give him my porridge, anyfink. I'll do anyfink to take this chance. I'll squeeze us both in somehow. But not Lizzie."

"Then I can't go," she said sadly.

"You *can*, Em'ly! Don't let me down. We'll fink of a way of fetching Lizzie later. Robin says I can be sure to get a job when I get to London, no bovver."

"What about him? Isn't he going?"

"No. He says he's got things to do here first. He's so kind, Em'ly. I know you don't like him much, but he really wants to help me to get away now, before Crick can get at me again. And he says there's a place for me on the coach definitely, if I can raise money. Please come wiv me."

Emily sighed. "No, Sam. Not without Lizzie."

"But, Em'ly!" he wailed. "We'd be free! Lizzie'd be all right for a bit. We could make some money and come back for her..."

"No," Emily said. "I'll give you what I've got. You can have it all. There's nothing to spend it on here. But I'm not going anywhere without Lizzie."

She broke away from him, running now, and she felt as if she was running through spiders' webs, breaking the threads as she ran.

"Fink about it!" Sam wailed after her.

All day she fretted about it, about the chance of leaving the mill for ever, leaving this wretched place behind and starting again in London. It might work. She might find a home somewhere, she might find a job in a Big House, she might be able to send for Lizzie to follow her. But what if it didn't work, and she was left to walk the streets and sleep in the gutters, no food, no home, nothing? No Lizzie. Even Bleakdale Mill was better that any of that. But what about Jim, all on his own in London? Shouldn't she go with Sam and try to find him and help him? He was too young to be all on his own.

But whatever she did, she knew that Sam was determined to go, and that nothing she said would make him change his mind. He had to take his chance, and she had to help him now because she had promised she would. On the way back from the mill that night, while Lizzie and Bess were chattering away about what exciting things might happen at the fair, she was worrying about how to get the money for Sam. He caught her eye as she was sitting down to eat, and his look was so anxious, so full of pleading, that she knew she had to help him. The day Crick had beaten him had been the worst day of his life, he had told her. Robin Small had promised to help him to take revenge, and surely flight was better than revenge? But she had no idea how she could get her money. She waited till Friday, and at teatime he kept glancing across at her with a look that was burning with hope. She pushed her bowl away, sick at heart. As soon as Mrs Cleggins went to her room for her own tea, Emily slipped after her. Nervously she knocked on her door. She heard a plate clattering, a jangle of cutlery, and then a voice called, "Who is it?"

"It's me, Mrs Cleggins. Emily Jarvis." Her hands were clasped together so tightly that she could feel her nails biting into her flesh.

"Can't I have a moment's peace?" Mrs Cleggins wrenched open the door. Emily caught sight of a comfortable armchair, a bright fire, a plate piled so high with meat and gravy that her stomach rumbled for it. Mrs Cleggins shut the door behind her and stood, arms folded. "What? What?"

"Mrs Cleggins, please could I have my wages money to take with me to the fair tomorrow?"

"What's going on? One of the other apprentices has asked for wages money too. You're supposed to be saving it for when you need new work clothes, new clogs. It's not to be frittered in fairgrounds."

Emily let her nails bite deeper into her palms. "Please, Mrs Cleggins. I might want a present for my sister. I might want to send money to my brother.

It's my money, Mrs Cleggins, and I've worked that hard for it and nearly broken my back with crawling about so long every day. And my work clothes are still too big for me because I've got thinner while I've been here, so they're going to last me till winter and I'll..." She could think of nothing more to say. "It is my money."

Mrs Cleggins had a quick temper and a sharp tongue, but she also had a sense of fairness. Besides, her meal was getting cold. "What's yours is yours," she said. "Wait." She opened her door again, letting the scent of rich stew curl round Emily for a moment as she went in. Then she came back with a small twist of rag. "Here. It's not everything you've earned. You need some for doctor's fees if you're ill, you know that, don't you? But take this, and don't spend it on nothing daft, and don't mither me again." And she slammed the door in Emily's face.

Emily could feel the coins through the rag, but she didn't want to see them or count them. She ran back to the schoolroom and gave it straight to Sam without looking at him, just pressed it into his hand and hurried back to sit by Lizzie. She put her arm round her sister and Lizzie looked at her, surprised.

"What's happened, Emily?" she asked. "You've gone all white."

"Nothing," said Emily. "I've been worrying about Jim, that's all. Worrying about what's happened to him, all on his own in London. At least we've got each other."

20

BUXFORD FAIR

Nobody slept much the night before the fair, and for the first time ever, they were all up and dressed before the morning bell went. The sky was light already. They clustered outside waiting for the carts to come. Emily wouldn't catch Sam's eye. She didn't want her day to be spoilt by saying goodbye to him.

"Will there be ribbons to buy?" Lizzie asked. "I'd love some ribbons for my hair. Will you buy some, Emily?"

Emily shook her head. "I don't know," she said. "There'll be ever such a lot to spend money on, I should think."

At last two carts bumped along the track. All the girls piled onto one, along with Skivvy; all the boys onto the other. Coaches arrived for Crick and two other overseers and Mrs Cleggins. The coach belonging to the Blackthorn family was the last to set off, with its two sturdy horses fitted out for the day with nodding red plumes fixed to their harnesses. The mill owner and his wife would be wanting to make quite a stir in Buxford. It was a bumpy journey, but nobody minded. Even if it had been pouring with rain they wouldn't have minded, but it wasn't; the sun was shining that day. As they drew near the town of Buxford they could hear the trumpets and drums of the fairground musicians, they could see the bustle of people, hear the high-pitched squeals of children, the calls of the muffin men and coffee sellers and the cries of the showmen. There were hot potato stalls, pease pudding stalls, sticky figs, and a steam-driven ride of prancing wooden horses with jangling bells and coloured reins. It was a glorious, thrilling, enticing cacophony of sound: "See Hairy Mary! See the Monster Twins. See Jimmy the Giant!"

"Oh, I wish our Jim was here with us!" Lizzie said. "'He'd have loved this, wouldn't he, Emily?"

Though they were bursting to be off exploring, they had to wait on the carts until the coaches from the mill arrived. Then the boys scrambled out of their wagon and surrounded the girls, grabbing their hands to pull them out till they were all screeching with laughter and excitement. Mrs Cleggins waved her arms at them and rushed over to tell them to behave, while the overseers stood with arms folded, scowling

"What's up with them?" Lizzie asked. "Aren't they excited too?"

"I think Mrs Cleggins is!" said Bess. "Look at her face! It's like a ripe tomato!"

At last the Blackthorn coach arrived, and Master Blackthorn was helped into his bathchair. "Roll me to the tea tent, Fergus." He twisted himself round as he was pushed past the apprentice children, and lifted his hand to them. There was almost the curve of a smile in his face, Emily thought. Mistress Blackthorn walked straight past as if she hadn't even seen them, as if they were nothing to do with her life at all, but Miss Sarah smiled round at them all.

"Have a lovely time, everyone!"

"And you, Miss Sarah!" Bess piped back. "And Master and Mistress too! And Fergus!"

"Where's Master Crispin?" Miriam asked. "I shall miss his smiling face!"

Dulcie laughed. "Aye, me an' all! He's got to be in charge of the mill today, hasn't he, as Master Blackthorn's here with us. Now he can really pretend he owns the place. He'll be that cheerful today!"

"I was going to ask him to dance!" Miriam said. "He makes me dance at my machine for twelve hours a day. Time he had a go!"

"Watch your tongue!" Mrs Cleggins snapped at her. "You could lose your job, saying things like that." She opened up a hamper and handed out the pies, wrapped in cloths and still warm. "Don't guzzle them straight away or you'll be hungry by dinnertime," she warned.

"Are you excited, Mrs Cleggins?" Bess asked.

Emily gave her a warning glance, but to her surprise, instead of snapping at Bess for asking such an impertinent question, the woman nodded. Something like a girl's smile flashed across her face and away again. "I am! I met Mr Cleggins at Buxford Fair," she said. "But that were a long time ago."

"Was he handsome?"

"He were good enough." Mrs Cleggins's eyes hazed over, then she bent down and rummaged inside her basket. "Here's sixpences Miss Sarah was kind enough to give you. Don't fritter it on rubbish, now. Cheap fairings don't last five minutes. And be back in cart by four o'clock or there'll be trouble, and I mean it." She hurried away before Bess could ask her anything else.

"You should not have asked her that," Skivvy said. The girls stared at her. Skivvy hardly ever spoke a word to them, just grinned her wet, gummy grin when she was ladling out their food.

"Why not?" Bess asked. "I was just curious."

"'Er husband, 'e died," Skivvy said. "Long time ago. There was a fire in mill at Buxford, and he died in it. Terrible thing, mill fire."

"How long did it take to burn down?" Robin asked. He had been lounging with Miriam and Dulcie against the side of the cart, teasing them both, but he turned his head, eyes full of concern and wonder, at Skivvy's story.

"No time at all. Cotton goes up in minutes. Flames come whooshing out of all them winders. Imagine! And black smoke so you can't see a hand in front of yer face. We was on top floor, me and 'er, spinners we were both, and I don't know how we got out, most of the girls up there perished. And 'er husband, 'e didn't know she was out, and 'e went in looking for her. So that's it. Now you know. Run off and enjoy yerselves."

"I can't now," said Bess, gazing at the distant figure of Mrs Cleggins making her way round the stalls.

"You can," Emily told her, determined. "It was a terrible thing, but it was all a long time ago, and we're here today to enjoy Miss Sarah's birthday present to us all, remember?"

"Yes. Poor Mrs Cleggins. But this is still the happiest day of my life!" Lizzie said.

"Mine too!" Bess forced herself to smile again. "My tummy's going all jiggly. There's so much to look at I don't know what to do first."

"Let's look at everything," Emily suggested. "And then decide."

"I definitely want a ride on one of those painted horses," Lizzie said. "And I want to buy some of those blue ribbons! Or red. Oh, and shall we go and see Hairy Mary?"

"She's covered in hair from head to toe, that's what the man said!" Bess giggled. "I should like to see her."

"And the dancing dolls! We must see them!" said Lizzie.

"Later, later," Emily laughed. She pressed her

sixpence inside her palm. I ought to give this to Sam, she thought. He'll need as much money as he can get hold of when he gets to London. And then she eyed the bright stalls and rides longingly and thought, *I'll just have a go on something, and I'll give him the rest when I see him.*

She ran after Lizzie. She was tired of worrying, always worrying. She just wanted to be like everyone else, enjoying herself. "Wait for me!" she shouted. "I don't want to miss anything."

Bess stopped, her eyes wide with wonder, and clasped Lizzie's arm. "What's that lady doing? Oh, ain't she beautiful! I want to see what she's doing."

A gypsy woman was sitting outside a striped awning, weaving her ringed fingers round and round over a glass ball. She was wearing bright, loose scarves with sparkling sequins set into them, and golden rings in her ears. And under a glittering headscarf her hair was black and loose and tumbling over her shoulders.

"Beautiful, she is," Bess sighed. "All them sparkly clothes! She looks like she's wearing stars!"

The woman caught her eye and beckoned the

three girls to come to her. "Tell your fortunes, darlings?" she said. "Put silver in my palm, and I'll tell you your future."

"My future?" Bess gasped. "Will I marry a rich man, and be taken away from the mill in a golden carriage, and live in a big house with hundreds of servants?"

"And have lots of children!" Lizzie giggled. "Go on, find out, Bess."

"No, Bess, don't spend all your money here," Emily said. "She's only got sixpence," she told the fortune-teller. "And it's to last her all day. Come on, Bess."

But still Bess lingered, enchanted by the dangling bells and ribbons that hung from the roof of the fortune-teller's tent, and by the dazzling coloured lights that reflected from the crystal ball on her felt-covered table.

The gypsy woman's voice was deep and lilting, as if she was singing to them "I won't read the crystal ball for nothing. I won't scry water for nothing, no I won't. Nor will I read cards. But I'll look at your palm for a farthing, and if you want to know more, you come back later, and that's kind of me, that is."

Lizzie stuck out her palm immediately, "Me first!"

"Let me see." The fortune-teller held Lizzie's hand in her own, screwing up her eyes. "I can see your life ahead of you," she said. "I can see your health, and your wealth. Give me a half penny and I'll tell you more."

"Me, no me!" Bess insisted, shoving her hand over Lizzie's.

The fortune-teller screwed up her eyes again, then looked at Bess, frowned, and shook her head, letting her hand drop. "No, child. I don't want to tell you your fortune."

"Aw, please," Bess begged. "Do you see a tall, handsome stranger?"

"Master Crispin!" Lizzie giggled.

"I see no marriage," the fortune-teller said abruptly. She looked at Emily, a strange, sad look in her eyes. "Take the child away, my darling. I don't want her money."

Suddenly alarmed, Emily pulled the girls away. Lizzie and Bess forgot about it in a moment; they rushed over to where a man was offering to show them his School of Educated Fleas, and Emily followed slowly, oddly disturbed. Then she saw Sam climbing up a ladder to a slide, and she stood to watch him. He waved to her from the top, unbalancing himself slightly, then launched himself onto the slide and careered down it, hooting loudly. He leapt off the bottom and ran up to her, panting.

"I just wanted one go at that!" he said. "It's the only thing I've spent money on. *Whoosh*, I went, like a bird, and I thought, this is you, Sam. This is you when you're free!"

"What's happening? You know, about the coach?" Emily asked urgently. She could shake him for his simple happiness. Didn't he know how frightened she was for him?

"It's all fixed! Robin said the coach leaves from the town cross at two. He's bought my place for me. I'm going home, Em'ly!"

She turned away, suddenly sad. "It's definitely going to happen then."

"Of course it is. There's still time for you to change your mind. Come with me! Please come!"

Lizzie and Bess were wandering around with a bunch of violets they had bought between them for Miss Sarah. When at last they spotted her they crept up behind her, daring each other to speak first.

"Miss Sarah," Lizzie said, nervous. Bess nudged her to say it again, and she tried several times before the mill owner's daughter stopped and looked round. Lizzie thrust the violets towards her.

"For me?"

"Happy Birthday, miss," the two girls chorused, and turned to run away, embarrassed now.

"Wait a minute! Don't run off so fast!" Miss Sarah called. "What are your names?"

"Lizzie Jarvis."

"You're one of our apprentice girls, aren't you? The girl with the auburn hair!"

"And I'm Bess Kelham, miss."

"Are you happy here?"

"Today, miss? It's my best day ever!" Bess said.

Miss Sarah laughed. "I mean, at our mill? Do you like it?"

For a moment the girls were silent – a beat too long. Then, "Yes, miss. Thank you," Lizzie faltered, and Miss Sarah looked down, fiddling with her gloves. The girls hesitated, not knowing what to do next, till Miss Sarah looked up again, smiling.

"Enjoy your day. Thank you for the flowers," she

said. And they ran off, chattering and giggling like starlings.

In the afternoon a band of fiddles and concertinas started to play the lively jigs and reels of country dancing. A space was cleared on the green and people began to get together to join in the sets. All the apprentice girls swirled and whirled with anyone who asked them. Sometimes the dance moved round in circles, so they didn't need a partner at all, they just had to hold hands with the people on either side. Emily and Lizzie laughed across at each other, breathless, bright with happiness. Emily glanced around at all the flushed faces of the other apprentices. They had become like a family to each other now. She knew them all, and it was the first time she had seen them all laughing together like this. She saw Robin, taller and more handsome than any of them, flamboyant as ever with his dazzling smile and wild, extrovert dancing. He twirled Miriam in his arms till she screamed for mercy, then put her down, bowed to her, and just stepped away leaving her without a partner at all. A moment later he was gone from sight.

Emily loosened her clasp on the two dancers

on each side of her and stepped back, watching for a moment, and then slipped away. She hurried towards the town centre, then down the main street. The church clock said two. There was the cross. And there was Sam, on his own, waiting anxiously and peering up and down the street. His face cleared the moment he saw her.

"You coming wiv me, then?"

She shook her head. "I just came to say goodbye, Sam."

He stuffed his hands in his pockets. *He has nothing*, she thought. *No spare clothes, no food, nothing to take with him to his new life.*

"Have you seen Robin?"

"No, no. He was dancing with Miriam, but I don't know where he is now."

"It don't matter. He said he didn't need to be here. It's all right. Coach will come, and I'll be away in no time." Sam was jittery with nerves, she could tell. So was she.

They waited ten more anxious minutes, not having a word to say to each other, listening through the strains of the dance music and laughter from the green, and at last they heard the rumble of wheels, the clatter of trotting hooves, and the cry of the coachman: "London coach!"

"Phew!" Sam blew out his cheeks. "It's come, Em'ly."

The coach pulled to a halt beside the cross, and Sam looked at Emily, awkward and shy. "I'd better get on it."

"You'd better. Bye then, Sam," she said. "Here. I bought you this," she said, shy. She thrust a wooden flute towards him. "You'll be happy, won't you?" She couldn't think of anything else to say or do, she felt so pleased for him, and so anxious. He stared back at her, just as tongue-tied as she was.

"Sam," she said suddenly. "Will you look out for Jim? Jim Jarvis? If you find him, tell him we're safe, will you?"

Sam looked back at her, one foot on the coach step. "Course I will! I'll do everyfink I can to find him."

He made to swing himself up, but the coachman looked down at him in surprise and held out his big red hand, barring his way. "Who are you, young man?"

"Samuel Jenkins."

"I'm expecting a tall lad," the coachman said.

"Robin Small?" Sam was stuttering now, and bright pink spots had appeared on his cheeks. "He fixed the ride for me."

"So where's your ticket?"

Sam looked at him helplessly. "He didn't give me one."

"Sam, he's here!" Emily called, then stopped, her hand on her mouth, and turned back, horrified, trying to warn Sam, because sure enough Robin was coming, but with him were two men in tall black hats. She knew immediately who they were; the overseers, Crick and Grimshaw.

Robin pointed towards Sam, and Crick gave out a roar of anger. He broke into a run and hauled Sam down from the steps of the coach, shaking him the way a dog would shake a rabbit.

"Trying to scarper? Trying to make a crafty getaway?" Crick kicked Sam's legs, and Grimshaw grabbed him by the arms, and they pinned him down on the ground.

"Away!" the coachman cried, and the horses stamped and whinnied and set off at a pace. Crick and Grimshaw were bent over Sam as he writhed on the ground, so they never saw what Emily saw; never saw kind, thoughtful Robin as he hopped smartly onto the coach and sat himself next to the driver, smirking. He lifted a hand slowly, regally, and doffed his cap at her.

21

CLOG DANCING

Emily pummelled Crick with her fists, trying to get him to stop kicking Sam, until he lashed out at her and threw her to the ground. Sobbing, she ran back to the green where the music was still playing and the dancers were still dancing, and she grabbed Miriam's arm.

"Get help!" she gasped. "Sam's hurt."

When they got back to the town cross Sam was lying on the ground, barely conscious. Crick was standing over him as if he expected him to get up and run away. Grimshaw was standing apart, watching out for Robin. Two of the older boys carried Sam to the wagon and laid him in the straw, and it was in sombre, frightened silence that the rest of the apprentices made their way back to Bleakdale.

When they got back to the apprentice house, Mrs Cleggins bathed Emily's face with stinking rags that had been soaked in herbs.

"You lied to me about needing that money. You'll work without wages for next three months," she told her grimly. "But I warned you, lass. Don't mess with Crick. I told you."

"I couldn't just stand and watch him kicking Sam like that," Emily tried to say, but it hurt her so much to speak that the words came out in a senseless mumble.

"You'll get your pretty face back, if that's what you're saying," Mrs Cleggins said. "Much use it will be to you here."

A few weeks later there were rumours that Robin had been captured soon after he arrived in London and had been brought back to Bleakdale. There was a ferment of excitement in the mill that day. Girls mouthed messages over the clatter of the machinery, fingers and hands mimed words, and gradually the story was told and understood. Robin Small had been captured in London. Who had captured him? Crick, of course. But why go after him? Why bring him back? Why bother?

"Where is he though?" Emily asked. "He's the one who needed beating up, not poor Sam."

"It wasn't his fault that Crick beat Sam up like that," Dulcie said.

"They say he was brought back at night, tied and gagged, and he's locked up in the basement with the rats!" said May.

"Serve him right if he is," Lizzie muttered darkly. "I hope the rats nibble his toes off."

"I hope he gets what he deserves," one of the older apprentices said. "I never liked him."

"You were the only one then," May said. "I think I would marry him, if he asked me, even now. I can't help it."

"Me too," said Miriam. "When he smiles at me, I go soft, I do."

Weeks passed, and it was all anyone talked about. What happened to Robin? Where was he now? Was he still alive? If they'd brought him back, why wasn't he working like the rest of them? Every day they watched out for him, expecting him to swagger in, smiling his dazzling smile at the girls, joking and laughing with the boys. "They found they couldn't do without me," they expected him to say. And then one day around Christmas he just appeared, thinner and paler than before, a silent ghost of his former self. He spoke to no one, smiled at no one, trudged to work and back with the rest of them, worked till his back was breaking and his feet had lost all feeling, coughed at night till you would think his lungs would burst; just like everyone else.

It was much worse for Sam. One of his legs had been broken, and his bones didn't set properly. He limped and shuffled like an old man, and he was always in pain. In the short time he was allowed to stay in bed while his leg was mending he practised his wooden flute, and when he was well enough to work he kept it tucked into his shirt. He played it on the way to and from the mill, and during Sunday free time. Emily could hear the piping from the shadow of the trees, like a bubble of birdsong. He promised Emily that on Christmas Day, he would play it in public. After the sumptuous Christmas meal of gruel with meat, he shyly produced it and stood up to play. Mrs Cleggins looked at him in astonishment, then gave a curt nod of her head. At first he could hardly play for smiling, but after a bit his confidence grew and he played not only the right notes in the right order, but at the right rhythm and speed, and a real tune emerged.

"Oh, I know this tune!" Mrs Cleggins said. "I used to clog to this when I worked at mill. Not that we needed music to dance to. We just copied noise of machines."

"Oh, go on, Mrs Cleggins. Dance it now," Bess said, clapping her hands.

"Certainly not!" the woman snorted. "Give Skivvy your bowls, and be quick about it."

"Aw, but it's Christmas!" Bess begged.

And suddenly it seemed that the music got the better of Mrs Cleggins. She stood looking straight ahead of her, arms at her side, and then began the tap, tap, tap of her clogs on the floor: rackety, rackety, rackety, like the clacking of machinery, rapid and rhythmic and insistent: rackety, rackety rack. Everyone stood up to see what her feet were doing. Bess dragged Lizzie off the bench they were sitting on to stand in the aisle. Then, as Sam played the music faster and faster, they too began to dance in their clogs. Mrs Cleggins's feet were flying and kicking, her cap was awry, her ruddy cheeks brighter than ever. Sam played the same tune over and over because he didn't know any other, but it didn't matter. Everyone was joining in, whistling or clapping or skipping, drumming their clogs, recalling the sounds they heard every working day, making them live: everyone, except Robin Small. He sat with his head in his hands, and when he looked up, there was no laughter in his face, no joy in the music, not even his old familiar look of scorn. It was as if he couldn't see or hear anything that was going on; as if he was seeing and hearing something else entirely, deep within himself.

As suddenly as she had started, Mrs Cleggins stopped. Her chest was heaving. The music stopped, the dancing stopped. She straightened her cap, and glared round at the mess the room had become, with its tables and benches pushed aside.

"You will tidy up now," she said, and swept out of the room.

Robin stood up and looked round at everyone. "You've turned into machines. The whole lot of you," he said.

22

Bess

In the deep winter weeks that followed, something happened that took all their minds off Robin Small. The weather was freezing over the New Year, and then the snow turned to rain and it was wet and damp and cold for days on end.

Emily and Lizzie had been working at the mill for a year; they could hardly imagine any other life now. All the children had become thin and pale, and many of them had bent backs and legs from the work they were doing, leaning over machines for hours on end to snatch at trailing cotton ends, or forever scrabbling round on the floor. Robin was right; they were machines.

It was Emily who first noticed that Bess was ill. Her bubbly laughter was hardly ever heard now; she spent most of the time coughing instead. She had dark rings like bruises round her eyes, and she seemed always tired, which wasn't like her. Nothing made her smile. She had no chirpy questions to ask or funny stories to tell. It was a struggle for her to work these days, and Crick was always there, watching her, shouting at her, pushing her, never giving her time to pause and catch her breath after a coughing fit.

"She's poorly," Lizzie told him, and was given a slap across the back with his stick for her insolence.

She kept an anxious eye on her friend, all the same. Even though it was so bitterly cold outside, the apprentices were still shooed out of the mill to eat their dinner. Lizzie draped her cloak across Bess's shoulders.

"Here. Have this," she said. "I'm roasting, Bess."

But Bess shook it off. She huddled up against a wall, trying to keep herself warm, and didn't seem to feel any warmer when she was in the apprentices' house.

"Never mind, it's Sunday tomorrow," Lizzie told her. "No work!"

"Ooh, I feel better already!" Bess gave her friend a weak smile. "No work, no Crick, no Master Crispin barking at us to go faster!"

Somehow she managed to get to church with the rest of the apprentices that day, trailing along, with Lizzie and Emily helping her arm in arm, but by the time she got home again she was coughing miserably. Mrs Cleggins noticed at last, and gave her a dose of something so fiery that her eyes watered. "That'll kill you or cure you, miss," she said grimly. "And I've seen a lot worse than you, child. But if you want to stop inside after lessons, you can. On your own, mind."

"I'd rather go to the den," Bess whispered to Lizzie. "Be nice and cosy in there."

"Perhaps you should keep warm by the fire," Lizzie suggested. "Warm your toes, Bess."

"We've got our rug to take down though. What could be warmer than that, Lizzie? I'll be snug as a rabbit with that round my feet!"

"It's not quite finished, but I'll bring it anyway."

When Mrs Cleggins wasn't looking Lizzie ran lightly upstairs to the girls' room and pulled from underneath her bed a plaited rug of cotton bits. In secret moments, and sometimes in the light of the moon in the bedroom, she and Bess had been weaving together scraps of cotton that they'd scavenged in the mill. It was meant to cover one of the logs to make it comfortable to sit on, but as soon as they crawled into the den Bess wrapped it round her knees, shivering. She sat hunched on the log with her eyes closed.

"You still like it here, don't you?" Lizzie asked anxiously.

Bess perked open her eyes. "Ooh, course I do! Best place in the world, this is! It's the fevvers that make it so pretty, ain't it? Makes me remember Miss Sarah, and the day she gave us letters to write. My bit of paper's still here, ain't it, next to yours?" She pointed up to where the papers had been festooned across the walls of twigs.

Lizzie frowned. The grass they had used for string had broken weeks ago in the winds that sometimes whirled inside the den. They had found the papers strewn everywhere, like white petals. "Yes," she nodded. "Still there, Bess. And the hedgehog still comes, look! Under his scrunchy bed of leaves, snoring like an old man!"

Bess smiled. "And the little mice come scuttling in. It's their house too, ain't it? I love it here."

Bess was always the last to get out of bed. She always had been, and Lizzie usually had to pull her out before Mrs Cleggins did it for her, much more roughly. Usually Bess made a joke of it, "Ooh, I could just do with a lie-in," she would say. "This bed's so comfortable!" But the morning after the visit to the den she just groaned deeply and murmured, "Please leave me here, Lizzie. I can't work today."

"Please get up," Lizzie said. "Are you very ill?"

"No. Not ill. Leave me, Lizzie."

By the time Bess finally got up, all the cloaks had gone from their hooks, including Bess's. She and Lizzie hunted under all the beds for it, and at last Mrs Cleggins forced them out of the door and told Bess she'd just have to run as fast as she could to dodge the raindrops. But Bess was too ill to run. Lizzie tried to share her own cloak with her, draping it over both their shoulders, and that made Bess laugh a little because their lantern shadow became a flapping beast. They splashed through the puddles in the streaming rain and arrived breathless and coughing. Bess's hair was flattened like rats' tails. Her frock and pinafore were soaked. She shivered all day, doing her best to keep up her scavenging, though sometimes when Crick had passed she just knelt on her hands and knees, heaving for breath, too tired to move. She got soaked again on the way back to the apprentice house because she kept wriggling away from the shelter of Lizzie's cloak. She went to bed in her damp shift, and shivered against the bony girl she was sharing with. During the night she took a fever, and by morning her eyes were red and swollen. She had lost her voice and could only produce a hoarse whisper. All the same, she was sent to work again. Her cloak had appeared just as mysteriously as it had vanished. It was obvious that one of the girls had decided to wear two cloaks the day before because it was so cold, but no one ever owned up to having taken it. Mrs Cleggins felt Bess's hot forehead, looked at her tongue, and said she was just about fit to work. Somehow she dragged herself through the day, shivering and hacking. She refused her breakfast and her dinner, and by the end of the day Lizzie and Emily had to help her back to the house in the sleet-filled rain. They took her straight upstairs and Lizzie climbed in bed next to her and put her arms round her to keep her warm. Emily sat on the opposite bed and tried to soothe them both with stories.

"She's so hot!" Lizzie whispered, frightened.

Emily felt Bess's hand. "Like a fire, she is," she

agreed. "Wet and hot and sticky. I'm getting Mrs Cleggins."

Mrs Cleggins clicked her tongue with annoyance and trudged up the stairs with a dose of vinegar and treacle, which made Bess retch. "Go down for your tea, you two girls. I'll let this one stay in bed just this once. If she's not better by morning I shall have to ask Master Crispin's permission to send for doctor, and he won't be pleased about that, I can tell you."

"But can I sleep with her tonight?" Lizzie asked.

"I daresay you can," Mrs Cleggins said. "If you want to catch it, whatever she's got. Go and fetch her some gruel now."

But Bess couldn't eat gruel, or anything else. Lizzie sat with her, holding her hand and whispering stories to her about the creatures that were living in the den.

"I expect Mister Hedgehog's having a nice old dream about worms and slugs," she said. "Where's Lizzie and Bess? he'll be saying to himself. It's lonely in here without them!"

"I like Mister Hedgehog," Bess murmured. "My granddad had a chin like that."

When the other girls came to bed and Mrs

Cleggins had locked them in for the night, as usual, and taken the lamp away, Lizzie snuggled up to Bess and tried to put her arms round her.

"You're burning hot," she said, afraid.

Bess tried to sit up. "Don't let them put me in the 'prentice graveyard."

"You'll get better when the doctor comes," Lizzie whispered back. Her voice was shaking. "I'll look after you."

"Please God, let her get well," she whispered to herself. "Please, oh please."

Just before dawn, Bess died. She went as quietly and quickly as a candle being blown out. Lizzie knew the moment it had happened. She felt her friend shudder and then lie completely still. She lay wide-eyed next to her, too afraid to move, too afraid to call out to Emily or to any of the other girls. When Mrs Cleggins unlocked the door in the morning she took one look at the still, white child and drew the bed cover over her face.

"God rest her soul. She had gumption, this little lass, and no mistake," was all she said.

The girls crept downstairs, mute with shock,

and were sent off to their work as if nothing had happened. They walked in silence, heads bowed, deep inside their own frightened thoughts. Emily put her arm round her sister, but Lizzie shrugged her away, too full of sorrow to speak, too afraid to cry. *Bess is dead.* That was all she could think about, all day. *My friend is dead. Bess.*

During the day Emily kept looking round for Lizzie. She was full of sorrow herself about Bess, but she knew how much worse it would be for Lizzie. Sometimes she caught sight of her as she emerged from under a machine, stony-faced, white with grief. She had lost her best friend, and it was unbearable for her. As soon as the bell rang for the end of the day Emily hurried outside to walk home with her and try to comfort her, but Lizzie had already run ahead of all the others up the long track to the apprentice house. She burst open the door and ran upstairs to the girls' bedroom.

The room was empty. Bess had gone.

Now Lizzie cried. Now she sobbed and beat her fists against the wall and flung herself on one of the beds until Mrs Cleggins hoisted her to her feet, lifted up her howling face and told her shush, she must stop, she must.

"Where's Bess? Where've they taken her?"

"She's buried."

Lizzie ran past her, grabbed her cloak off the pegs, and hurtled down the stairs and straight out of the door, pushing past Emily and the others, wild with grief.

"Mrs Cleggins, please let me go after her," Emily begged. "Please let me find her and bring her back."

But Mrs Cleggins locked the outer door firmly and stood with her back against it. "I cannot let you wander about in the dark as well," she said firmly. "You could fall in river, or millpond, or be dashed to bits in millrace. Get to bed. I'll leave lamp on door nail, so child will make her way back safe. I'll hear her knocking on door. Get upstairs, pray for dead. It's all you can do."

In the bedroom, Emily wrenched back the shutters and stared out at the black hill, the black bony trees, the black rain, the black black night. She was sick with terror at the thought of Lizzie wandering about on her own out there.

"Lizzie, Lizzie, where are you?" she sobbed. "Lizzie, come back."

23

THE LOST CHILDREN

Lizzie scrambled along the edge of the riverbank, feeling her way by memory in the stifling darkness. She ran into the little den that she and Bess had made, but she had no thoughts of staying there. She grabbed their cotton rug and felt around for a couple of goose feathers and bits of paper; anything she could find from their special place that Bess had loved so much. Then she scrambled out again and ran on. Now the river path was overgrown with brambles that snatched at her cheeks and her hair, like bony fingers with sharp, malevolent nails. Trees grew all around, and now their twisted branches reached out to her as if they were bone-white arms trying to draw her into their embrace. Now and again, the moon broke through the clouds and shone with a peculiar misty pallor, lighting her way to the patch of ground where the dead apprentice children were buried. She saw immediately that a mound of earth had been recently turned. She ran over and knelt down by it.

"I've come to keep you company, Bess," she whispered. "Cos you're scared to be here on your own. And look, I've brought our little rug for you, to keep you warm."

She laid the plaited cotton rug on the mound, and tucked the feathers and parchment scraps into its folds.

"Just like our den now," she whispered. "Like our own palace."

Deep night drew in, cold dropped down. In the valley, foxes barked. All around her, creatures scuttled in the undergrowth. It seemed to Lizzie now that small white figures were darting between the trees, light as air: here, and now there, here again, pale flickers of formless light.

"Are you the lost children?" she whispered.

Something sent a shivery cry across the night; something else answered. A pause, and there it came again. *Owls, it's owls.* Lizzie told herself, but the cries came again, now up there, now over there, all around her; like the helpless sound of children crying.

"There Bess. All the lost children have come to

look after you. You mustn't be scared, cos you ain't on your own now, see?" Lizzie pulled her cloak around herself and lay down, shushed and soothed at last by the sighing of the wind.

Miss Sarah was being driven home that night after visiting a friend in Oldcastle. She was gazing out of the carriage window, dreamily thinking about her friend's very nice brother, when she thought she glimpsed a small figure flitting along the bank on the other side of the river. She asked the driver to stop for a minute and stepped down from the carriage. Holding her lantern high, she went to the edge of the river and stood on the rickety old bridge that spanned it. Below her, the water that powered her father's mill churned and spat like a black rearing beast of the night. Clouds were racing across the moon, trees bending and flashing their gleaming white branches.

That's what I saw, she told herself. *Just trees in the moonlight. And it's far too cold to be standing here in the dark. Home, Sarah, and hot supper, and bed.*

She went back towards the carriage and stood

near it, gazing again into the blackness beyond the river.

"Is something wrong, Miss Sarah?" the carriage driver asked.

"No. It's fine. Carry on." Yet the glimpse of that pale *something* haunted her; she couldn't shake off the thought that it might have been a child. If it was, what was a child doing out there on the riverbank on its own, at that time of night?

At home, a bright fire was blazing. Her parents and brother were waiting up for her to dine with them. She was restless and anxious, too uneasy to settle to their conversation. Master Blackthorn was jovial because he had just received the latest shipment of cotton from the West Indies at a very good price.

"I'm purchasing from a different plantation," he told them, rubbing his hands together. "It was an excellent decision, Crispin."

"It's to be hoped slaves are treated well there," Sarah said abruptly.

"Slaves treated well!" her brother repeated scornfully. "What an idea, Sarah. You don't buy slaves to treat them well. You buy them to work."

"Enough!" their mother said sharply. "Enough.

We don't talk about slaves at the supper table. It gives me indigestion."

But Sarah wouldn't let the subject drop. "You must know how badly slaves are treated. Newspapers are full of it!"

"You're being very rude to your father," her mother whispered.

"My sister reads too much and understands too little," Crispin said.

"Our country thrives on the cotton industry. We are a great nation. I'm proud to be part of it," Mr Blackthorn said. "There, let it drop, my dear."

"And I'm afraid mill workers are treated just as badly," Sarah muttered. She bit her lip. She had never been so outspoken before, yet she kept remembering the dark river, remembering the ghost glimpse of a child running in the night. She couldn't shake the image away. She blundered on helplessly. "I feel so sad for them, when I see them trudging home after work every day – especially the little apprentice children. You must have seen how frightened they are, and how tired."

Her mother waved her hand at her to stop, stop now. "Frightened! Oh, Sarah! What an idea! I've never seen anything of the sort."

Perhaps that's because you don't want to, Sarah's look said, though she held her tongue this time.

"It's none of your business how the workers are treated," Crispin snapped. "Running the mill is a man's job, not a soft-hearted woman's!"

Her father mopped his mouth with his napkin. "Come, my dear. Let's not quarrel, today of all days. We bring work to these people, remember? Wages! Let's have a toast to Bleakdale Mill, the heart of the community!"

Sarah stood up. "Excuse me. I'm not hungry any more."

She went up to her room and paced around, too angry to sew or to read. She heard her mother going up to her own room. She heard her father and Crispin laughing together in the study. Her maid came in to trim the lamps and Sarah said abruptly, "Hetty, what's on the far side of the river?"

"Over beyond, miss? Nowt."

"Are you sure? There's a bridge. It must lead to somewhere."

Hetty lowered her voice. "Only 'prentice graveyard, miss." She turned to leave the room, but

Sarah called her back abruptly.

"Will you fetch your cloak and mine? I want us to go out."

"Out, miss? At this time of night?"

"I need air. I need a walk."

"Walk, miss?" repeated Hetty limply. "Wherever to?"

"I think I need to go to that graveyard."

Hetty whimpered, but she fetched the cloaks. They slipped quietly out of the house and down the track that led away from the mill and its buildings. When they came to the old bridge the maid hesitated, clutching her cloak around her. "I don't like to go no further, miss."

"Neither do I. But I think we have to."

They walked in silence over the bridge and along the scrubby track next to the river. By the time they reached the graveyard Hetty's eyes were nearly starting out of their sockets in terror of the owls hooting so close to her, and the scrabbling of creatures around her feet, and the startling white of the moonlight on the trees. She remembered the crying sounds at night; she remembered the stories of the lost children. Her mistress marched grimly ahead of her and broke through to the patch of mounds and humps that had to be the apprentices' graveyard. She walked slowly through it, her lantern raised high, and saw a child lying on the ground.

Hetty gasped. "It's one of our 'prentices," she whispered. "I can tell by her smock."

As they approached her, Lizzie sat up, startled by the light of the lamp, and scrambled to her feet. Sarah caught her before she ran away.

"Wait, little one. What are you doing here?"

Lizzie wrapped her arms round herself, shivering. "I was keeping Bess company. So she wouldn't be afraid."

Sarah looked at the mound of damp soil and nodded, understanding everything. She crouched down next to Lizzie. "Is this where she is?" She patted the earth, and Lizzie nodded.

"It's Bess, miss."

"Bess? Your friend?" Sarah put her arms round Lizzie and sat with her, rocking her gently, while Hetty hopped from one leg to the other, trying to keep herself warm.

"She's asleep," Sarah said at last. "Will you carry her, Hetty? I'll take the lantern, and if she gets too heavy you must pass her over to me."

Hetty was built like a carthorse, and Lizzie was thin and light. The maid lifted her up and carried her with no trouble at all, stumping fast through the trees to be away from the dreadful place where children of the mill were buried without names to be remembered by. When they came to the mill owner's house Sarah asked Hetty to take Lizzie straight up to the servants' bedrooms in the attic.

"Keep her warm tonight. Tomorrow, wake her up in good time to start her shift at mill. She mustn't be late. I shall tell Mrs Cleggins we found her in the dark, and it was too late to wake up the apprentice house. I'll make sure she isn't punished. Poor child." She looked at Lizzie now in the light of the house lamp; she saw the tumble of her autumn-bronze hair. "I know this little one," she said sadly. "I remember her friend. Take care of her tonight, Hetty."

24

THE TERRIBLE ACCIDENT

It could be that Lizzie never really got over losing Bess, or ever recovered from the night she spent out on the moor watching over her. Spring came again and the woods were full of the laughing cries of green woodpeckers. High up in the trees rooks built their nests, and the ground below them was carpeted with bluebells. The children went to work in daylight, and came out to find the sun still shining; but Lizzie never went back to the den that she and Bess had made, never joined in the clogging or singing that cheered up the other children in their free time. She would sit by herself, watching, dreaming. Sam sat by her sometimes, playing made-up tunes on his flute, making up jokes to tease a smile out of her, and she would just stare at him as if she wasn't quite sure who he was any more. On Sundays she would walk silently over to Oldcastle church and back as if it was the same trudge that she took to the mill on all the other days; nothing different or special about it any more.

"We've had seventy-two Sundays here now," Emily told her, trying to cheer her up. "Guess how many more there will be before our apprenticeship ends?"

Lizzie shrugged. What did it matter?

"Well, I've no idea!" Emily laughed. "I don't think I can count that far! Work never gets better, my back never stops aching, I'm coughing like an old man; but for seventy-two whole days I've been happy! That's good, isn't it, Lizzie?"

Deep inside her, Emily often wondered whether Lizzie would ever be happy again. Her sister was so tired and listless; she worked in a trance, stooping, scrambling, scavenging, stooping, scrambling, scavenging; by the end of every day she was nearly asleep. And it was because she was so tired that she had her terrible accident.

It happened in late May, the loveliest day of the year. Work that day seemed to go on for ever. Wheels whirring within wheels, cogs grinding within cogs, threads skimming, fluff floating; nobody spoke, or mimed, or clog-danced at their machines. They wanted to be outside to feel the sun on their faces. The long, long day trundled on interminably.

At last the bell for the end of the apprentices' day was rung, and Lizzie, drowsy with tiredness and boredom, straightened up from under her machine half a second too soon. Instantly her apron strings were snatched by the moving carriage. She screamed, desperately trying to tug herself free, but the movement of the carriage was too strong, too rapid. She was dragged to the back of the machine, dragged forward to the front, dragged back again, her legs and arms flailing uselessly. She writhed and kicked, and nobody noticed; back again, thumped and thudded along the floor, her apron hopelessly tangled in the machine as it was pulled tighter and tighter. She couldn't release herself or scream out, she had no air in her lungs, no strength left. Finally she lost consciousness and was thumped to and fro like a rag doll.

At last, Flo saw what had happened and ran screaming for Crick. Somebody else ran to find Emily. Crick arrived, cursing and bellowing at Lizzie for her carelessness, for the spilt blood, for the lost time, for the ruin of work. He pulled the lever to stop the machine and Flo and Emily crawled underneath it and struggled with trembling fingers to release Lizzie from the trapped apron.

"Oh, Lizzie! Lizzie!" Emily sobbed. "Look what's happened! Oh, look at you!"

Lizzie had to be cut free, and then she was dragged out from under the machine and laid on the floor. Workers clustered round her and were sent back to their machines. "It isn't time yet!" Crick shouted.

"Is she alive?" Flo mouthed.

"I don't know. I don't know," Emily moaned. She stood up, looking round helplessly. "We should get her out of here, it's so hot and noisy."

She and Flo between them carried Lizzie across the room, winding between the machines and the gawping workers. Crick paced the floor, his eyes black and steely. Nobody dared stop to help them. Slowly, carefully, they carried her downstairs, and put her on the floor again. Emily could hardly see what she was doing because of the tears streaming down her cheeks.

"I must go back," Flo said. "Crick'll sack me else."

Emily nodded. She gazed round helplessly, then

saw some wheeled pallets, parked ready to collect bales of cotton from the wagons. Now she knew exactly what to do. She wheeled one to where Lizzie was lying. The child was as white as the cotton itself. Tenderly, Emily lifted her sister onto the pallet and pushed it out of the building, expecting at any moment to hear a roar of fury from Crick. She struggled with it along the dusty track and into the cobbled yard of the mill owner's house. Who would be there? Master Crispin? Mrs Blackthorn? But there was no time to be afraid of them. No time to think. She ran up the steps and banged on the front door with both her fists. A maid opened it a crack and then tried to close it again, astonished to see one of the mill girls standing there in the middle of the afternoon.

"I want to see Miss Sarah," Emily sobbed, pushing against the door with all her strength.

There was something in her voice, something in the shock of grief in her face, that caused the maid to open the door properly. She saw the bloodstained child lying on the wooden pallet, put her hand to her mouth, and then hurried to the room where Sarah and her brother were reading newspapers.

"Miss Sarah, there's one of mill girls wants to see you. One of 'prentices."

Master Crispin shook his newspaper. "Send her back to work at once," he growled. "What does she think she's doing?"

"Looks like there's been an accident," the maid gasped. "Looks like there's been a death."

In seconds Miss Sarah was at the door. She ran down to Emily and gazed with horror at Lizzie's pale face.

"It's that child again!"

"She's Lizzie, miss," Emily said. She could hardly speak for fear.

"What happened? Did you see it?"

Emily shook her head. "I wasn't there. She got caught up beneath a spinning machine when she was scavenging. Her apron got trapped." She was tangling her own apron strings in her hand, wrenching them tight, hardly knowing what she was doing or saying.

Master Crispin had come down the steps to join them, his newspaper still in his hand. "Why are these children so careless?" he asked irritably. He put the back of his hand on Lizzie's forehead. "She's very cold." He glanced at Emily. "You'd better get back to your machine."

"Some things are more important than cotton," his sister said sharply. She knelt down and felt for Lizzie's hand, trying to find a pulse.

"Miss," Emily whispered. "Is she...?" But she couldn't finish the question; she was too afraid.

"We'd best not lift her, had we?" Miss Sarah asked her brother.

"Best not. I'll send for the doctor, if it's not too late." Master Crispin straightened up. "We can wheel her round the back and bring her in through the kitchen, to avoid stairs. You stay with her. I must go and ask Crick what happened." He glanced again at Emily. "I've told you, lass. Get back to your machine. There's nothing you can do here."

Emily clutched back the sobs in her throat and edged away. She watched helplessly as servants ran from the house. Then Lizzie was wheeled away from her round the back of the house, out of sight.

25

No News for Emily

Two hours later, Dr Oxton arrived on horseback. He was an elderly man, severely stooped like a wind-blown tree, and when he took his stumbling steps into the house and up the stairs anyone might have thought he needed a doctor himself. He was used to coming to Bleakdale to give advice on doses of medicine for sickly children. Sometimes he cured them, sometimes he didn't, but whenever he came he glowered at the dark mill buildings and said, "That mill is no place for children, sick or well." His voice was a deep, disappointed rumble in the back of his throat.

In spite of the hot day, Hetty had covered Lizzie with a warm blanket. She and Miss Sarah sat with her in the kitchen, one either side of her, holding a limp hand. The doctor shook his head when he saw the state Lizzie was in.

"You, at least, have a spot of humanity, Miss

Blackthorn. You've brought a dying child into your house."

Sarah gave a sob of despair. "Please, Dr Oxton, don't say that. Surely you can save her?"

"I'm a doctor, not a miracle worker. She's in a very bad way."

"Poor little Lizzie."

"Do you know the lass?" he asked.

She nodded. "I do, a little."

"I could send her to hospital, but it's a very long way and a very rough journey from here. It wouldn't do her any good just now to be bumping over those cart tracks."

"She must stay here then," said Sarah. "We'll do what we can."

"I've no medicine to help her. I can splint her bones; they'll mend in time. The blood is not a problem; you can clean her up and she'll not bleed again, if she's kept still. But her spirit has received such a terrifying shock that she has fallen into a deep coma. You can see that. If she's to stay here, she must be looked after day and night. She must be kept warm and comfortable, but more than that, she must be soothed out of her nightmare.

If you can do that in this godforsaken place, then there's a chance that the child's will to live might return."

"We'll try," said Sarah. She looked at Hetty. "Won't we?"

Hetty wiped her eyes on her apron and nodded. "God bless the child, she'll not go back to that graveyard, Miss Sarah."

A bed was made up in Sarah's room, and Lizzie was carried carefully upstairs. Doctor Oxton supervised the cleaning of the wounds, the wrapping of bandages, the splinting of limbs and the pressing of a sponge of cold water to Lizzie's lips, while Lizzie lay in a deep, silent sleep. After a supper of good meat and wine he shambled his bent way out of the house and rode back home.

There was a deep, hopeless silence in the room after the doctor had left. Sarah drew back the heavy curtains, letting what was left of the day's sunlight into the room. Her mother came in and looked aghast at the child in the truckle bed.

"Have you taken leave of your senses?" she asked. "Mill children are always falling ill. Do you want to turn this house into a hospital?"

Sarah touched Lizzie's hair. "I know her. I can't just let her die, Mother."

"I can't imagine what your father and your brother will have to say about it. Bringing a mill child into the house, into your own room!"

"Then they needn't know," said Sarah. "Crispin probably won't even ask."

"If he does, I'll tell him Dr Oxton has taken her away with him. Remember that, Hetty. I wish to goodness he had, and saved us all this bother." Her mother swept out of the room, and Sarah sank down on the chair next to Lizzie's bed.

"I'm glad he didn't," she murmured. She looked up at Hetty. "I feel so drawn to this little one, Hetty. She seems to keep coming into my life. I must help her, mustn't I?"

"You must look after yourself first, that's what you must do," said Hetty firmly. "I'll fetch you some supper, and when it's full dark, I'll sit with her, and you can sleep. You'll need all your strength for this. We both will."

Emily spent the next week in a trance of weariness and despair. She was so worried about Lizzie that she couldn't sleep at night, and in the day she stared, mesmerised, into the clanking arms of her machine. *So it will be, day after day and year after year*, she thought. *I'll be like all the other girls, all the women, there will never be anything else for me in life. And if Lizzie has died, then everything I loved has been taken away from me.*

She watched Master Crispin as he strolled through the mill sheds. Once he came right up to her machine. *He's going to speak to me about Lizzie*, she thought. But he didn't. He passed on, eyes glinting. "Master Crispin!" she called. "Please, Master Crispin?" He paused for half a second, just catching the high sound of a girl's voice behind him. He turned his head, not even recognising her, and waved his hand irritably to her to get on with her work.

"I've no idea where Lizzie is. I've no idea whether she's recovered, whether she's alive even," she said to Sam in the dinner break. "And I daren't go to Miss Sarah's house and ask."

"But you must ask. I'll go with you," Sam said. "I'll go for you, if you like."

Emily shook her head. "Master Crispin would be angry," she said. "I know he would. I'm so frightened of him, Sam. And Mrs Blackthorn. I'll find out somehow, but I'll not ask at the front door."

Instead, whenever she had the chance, she hung round near the kitchens. She turned up very day, and was ignored. One evening she saw Hetty standing in the yard, yawning and stretching as if she'd been up all night, and she took the chance to run up to her.

"Excuse me," she said. "Can you tell me about Lizzie?"

Hetty folded her arms. *Now what?* she thought. *If I tell the truth, this girl and goodness knows who else from the 'prentice house will be round every day asking after the child. Miss Sarah's secret will be out, and she'll be in trouble with her mother, no doubt, who's pretending she doesn't know what's going on. And I'll be in trouble too.*

"What about her?" she asked slowly, trying to get her mind round the problem.

"Is she...?" And still Emily couldn't ask the question. "How is she?"

Hetty caught a glimpse of Master Crispin striding across the yard, and she made up her mind quickly. "Dr Oxton took her away," she said. *After all, those were the very words Mrs Blackthorn had told me* to use, she thought. *I'm just repeating them in his presence.* "She's in good hands," she added out of kindness because Emily looked so stricken. Then she went back into the house, closing the kitchen door firmly behind her. She stood with her back to it, trying to calm herself. "That was a sin, Hetty Gamble," she told herself. "That poor lass is beside herself with worry. But what is there to tell her? Lizzie's in such a deep sleep, not moving, not eating, not speaking, nothing; she might as well be dead. Better for that lass to have hope, than to know what's really going on."

"What did you find out?" Sam asked Emily. He had been standing at a distance with Miriam, jigging from foot to foot with impatience, waiting for her to walk away from the cobbled yard.

She shook her head. "Nothing really. Doctor took her away with him, that's all I know."

"Then he'll have taken her to the 'ospickal!" he said, brightening up. "She'll be back in no time, fit as a flea."

"And working under the very machine that tried to eat her up," Miriam said.

Sam frowned at her, and Miriam shrugged. "It's

true though," she said. "She's better off out of it, wherever she is."

"Better off away from Cruel Crick, any time," Sam agreed. "And Robin says there should be metal guards on them machines, anyway."

"Oh, don't listen to him!" Miriam laughed. "He made a right fool of you, Sam Jenkins." She wandered away. Whatever she said about Robin Small, she would give anything for him so smile at her again, to whirl her around in a country dance like he had done at the fair. She could see him now, talking to some other lads, the centre of the ring. *He's back*, she thought. *He's turning into his old self again. Maybe he'll notice me and look at me special, like he used to.*

"Sam, don't have anything to do with him," Emily begged. "He's a liar and a cheat. He did you out of all your money!"

"He's promised me he'll make up for it," Sam muttered. "And anyway, he saw that there was still a place on the coach after I was dragged off it, and he took a chance himself. That's what happened, Em'ly."

Emily sighed with impatience. "You'd believe

anything he tells you, Sam. You're under his spell, like all the rest of them."

"Well, this is something else he tells me, and I do believe this. That it's Master Crispin and Master Blackthorn who robbed me, not him. If they ran this place better, we wouldn't have tried to get away from it. Bess wouldn't have died. Lizzie wouldn't have had that accident." He blew out his lips. "That's what Robin is saying. He's got a plan for revenge, he says. And I'm part of it!"

Before Emily could say anything else, he darted away from her because Robin had raised his arm and whistled to him, as if he were a dog.

Emily was weary to the bone, weary to the heart. All she wanted to do was lay down her head and sleep. When at last the girls were sent up to their room she could hardly climb the stairs, but no sooner had she rolled onto her bed than she was tossing and turning, fretting again about Lizzie, fretting about Sam. What if he did something stupid? Whatever it was that Robin was planning, he would stand back and let Sam take the blame for it, she was sure of that. But even more than her concern about Sam was her worry about Lizzie. Mrs Cleggins told her the same thing as Hetty had told her: "Dr Oxton has taken her away with him. That's all I know." Surely the doctor wouldn't just take her away and not let anyone know what had happened to her? Miss Sarah would know something, even if her maid didn't.

On her way to the mill every day she kept her eyes fixed on the Blackthorn house, hoping to catch a glimpse of Miss Sarah in one of the windows. She sometimes heard a squawk of hens and once caught sight of Hetty's blue frock in the yard. She'd tried to break away from the hurrying line of the other mill girls, but was hauled back into place by Crick, his grip like a vice on her elbow. All day while she was working she kept glancing over her shoulder. She had decided that if she saw Master Crispin again she would take the courage to speak to him. Maybe, one day, Miss Sarah would be with him. She did come in occasionally. If she did, she would surely recognise Emily and give her a reassuring smile. That was all she needed. But the days dragged on, and no one came from the Mill House.

26

WHERE AM I?

Hetty and Sarah had been taking it in turns all week to sit with Lizzie. Mrs Blackthorn never came into the room; she had decided that she knew nothing at all now about the child. She'd received an enquiry from Mrs Cleggins from the apprentice house and responded that the child was in the doctor's care. She convinced herself that Dr Oxton had indeed taken her away. If she saw Hetty or her daughter coming up the stairs to the room with bowls of water she simply looked away. It was her job to keep her husband and son fed and happy; it was their job to keep Bleakdale Mill going. What Sarah did with her own time was of no concern to her.

It was on Hetty's shift at the bedside, several weeks after the accident, that Lizzie emerged from her coma. She felt as if she was wrapped in cobwebs; tight strands that bound her legs together, that pressed her arms to her sides, and kept her eyelids shut and her mouth tight closed. She tried to speak, and couldn't. She tried to break herself free of the cobwebs, and couldn't; the strands were too tight, the effort was too great. She tried to shake herself out of the darkness, but it was too deep. She slipped back into safe, quiet sleep. It was some hours before she woke again. She felt herself rising out of swirls of darkness. Her eyes slowly opened and found light.

Hetty was dozing beside her, holding her hand, when she suddenly felt the hand twitch and opened her eyes to find Lizzie staring at her.

"Where am I?" Lizzie asked.

"Oh, Lizzie!" Hetty gasped. "You're awake! You're better! Are you better? Don't move! Keep still! Oh my word, are you really better?"

Lizzie kept staring at her. "Where am I?" she asked again.

"You're in Miss Sarah's room!"

"Miss Sarah?"

"Miss Blackthorn." Hetty kept rubbing Lizzie's hand as if it still needed warming. "She's been looking after you."

"Miss Blackthorn?" Lizzie frowned. "Who's Miss Blackthorn?" She closed her eyes and went to sleep again, but it was a natural sleep, Hetty could tell. She was no longer in a coma. Her cheeks had lost the white pallor of death, and her eyelashes fluttered slightly as if she was just held in a light dream. When she dared, Hetty let go of her hand and ran to find Sarah, who was sitting sewing downstairs.

"She's been awake! She's been talking!" she whispered. "I do believe the child is going to live!"

Lizzie woke again from a sweet dream of long ago, of sitting in firelight with a woman and a boy and a girl. She didn't know who they were, but they made her feel safe. She opened her eyes and stared round the strange room, puzzled. She couldn't remember anything that had happened to her. She had no idea why she was lying between clean sheets in a room that was the colour of green apples. She was aching all over, and when she struggled to sit up she saw that her one of her arms was tightly bound so she couldn't move it at all, and that her skin was purple and yellow with bruises. She had no memory of being thumped backwards and forwards like a rag doll under a moving machine. Carefully she eased herself out of bed, and saw that one of her legs was as bruised as her arm. At that moment the door opened and a fair-haired young woman came in and ran to her, her face lit with joy and concern.

"Lizzie! Lizzie! You really are awake! Don't you dare try to get out of bed! Lie back down at once!"

Another woman came in, the hefty woman in the blue dress who had been sitting by the bed earlier. She carried a bowl of water, which she placed on a polished dresser near the window.

"Shall I wash her or shall you, Miss Sarah?" she asked. "And one of us should get some food down her now, and another one of us should send word to Dr Oxton and ask him what we should do next now she's alive."

"You wash her," the young woman said. "I'll do the other things." She bent over Lizzie, smoothing her hair away from her eyes, smiling down at her. "How do you feel, child? "

"Where am I?" Lizzie asked.

The large woman laughed. "That's all she'll say! *Where am I? Where am I?* I told her, you're in Miss Sarah's room, and she said, 'Who's Miss Sarah?' She's half asleep still, God bless her."

"I'll fetch her something warm and light from the

kitchen," Sarah said. "And then I'll send a message to Dr Oxton. It feels as if a miracle has happened, doesn't it, Hetty?" She pulled back the curtains to let in the full summer sunlight, and left the room.

"You'll feel better for a wash," Hetty told Lizzie. "Then I've got some nice ointment to put on those bruises, though my ma always swore by a lump of beef. Mind you, if we were to put a bit of beef on all those bruises you'd look like a butcher's shop." Her breath came hissing through her teeth as she lifted away the last of Lizzie's bandages. "Poor lass. Gave yourself a good thumping, you did."

"What happened?"

"You had an accident at work, that's all I know."

Lizzie frowned. "Work? What work?"

Hetty sat back, her blue eyes wide with amazement. "You really don't know, do you? You don't know who you are, or where you are, or what's gone on. Well, it's better if you forget, except for your name, and that's Lizzie, I'm told. Miss Sarah can tell you more if she wants to. Now close your eyes because I'm going to swab a wet flannel across your face, and I've never met a child yet who likes having that done to them."

For the next few days Lizzie saw no one except Hetty and Miss Sarah, who sometimes read to her, and sometimes just sat with her, chatting or sewing. An old, bent man called Dr Oxton came and examined her and rumbled that she could get out of bed a little every day, and that they must be careful with her right arm, which was broken, but it would mend soon.

"But her heart isn't mended, and neither is her mind. Don't say anything to frighten her. And try not to send her back to that place," he told Sarah, and she shook her head.

"I've no intention of doing that, Doctor," she said.

"What did he mean?" Lizzie asked Hetty later. "What place?"

But Hetty just lifted her apron and wiped her eyes. "One day, you'll remember," was all she said.

Gradually Lizzie began to be able to do things for herself, feed and wash herself with one arm, get herself out of bed and wander round the room. She would touch the objects on the shelves and the mantelpiece: china ornaments, a vase with roses painted on it. On the wall was a framed sampler worked in colourful stitching. She couldn't read the words, and Hetty told that she couldn't either, except for *Sarah Blackthorn, 1859* stitched at the bottom.

"Miss Sarah would have been about ten years old when she did it," she told Lizzie. "But I was never taught to do anything like that. Were you, Lizzie?"

"I don't know," Lizzie said flatly. "I don't remember."

"No," said Hetty. "I'm sorry, Lizzie. Of course you don't remember."

Lizzie turned away, as upset as Hetty. She gazed out of the window at the great flank of black hill rising away from the house like a bruised cloud. She could hear the rushing sound of the river, and she could see in the distance a gaunt building with its hundreds of blank windows; but nothing that she saw made any sense to her. Twice a day she heard the thundering *rat tat tat* of men, women and children clattering to and from the big building. *Who are they? Where are they going? What are they doing?* she asked herself. *Do I have anything to do with that?* She thought, sometimes, that maybe she did, but it hurt her head to try to think about it. Once she saw a girl stop and turn her white face towards the house, scanning the windows as if she was looking for something or someone. Lizzie would have liked to wave to her, but instead she stood back behind the curtain, shy.

Every night Miss Sarah came into the room and helped her to bed, smoothed back her hair with her cool hands, read to her and left again with a rustle of her green taffeta dress. And always Lizzie puzzled to herself, *Who is she? Does she have anything to do with me?*

She took the courage to ask her just that, once when they had been laughing together and felt at ease with each other. "Who are you?"

"I'm your friend," the lady had said, smiling down at her. "You can call me Sarah."

"She's Miss Sarah, Master Blackthorn's daughter," Hetty said firmly, when they were alone again. "She's been looking after you."

It didn't help. Nothing made sense; nothing was familiar. When Lizzie tried to look into her past she felt numb and afraid; her memories were swirls of fog, revealing nothing.

One day, after the old rumbling doctor's weekly

visit, Sarah came into the room and said cheerfully, "Good news, Lizzie! Dr Oxton says you're well enough to leave now."

Lizzie looked at her in panic. "But where shall I go? I don't know where to go!"

"Well, you're not going anywhere on your own. I have a plan!" Sarah clapped her hands together. "The doctor tells me the sea air will do you the power of good, and I know just the right place to take you! My aunt has a house right on the sea front in the Wirral, and I love to go there every year about this time. Would you like to come with me?"

"I don't think I've ever seen the sea," Lizzie said.

"Well, we can put that right! It's a long way, and we may have to stop somewhere overnight so you don't get overtired, but when we arrive you will be in the most beautiful place in the world! I spent my childhood there, and I love it. The weather is much kinder over in the west. The sun and the sea air will make you well and strong again, I know they will. I'll get Hetty to pack a bag for you, and look, Lizzie – what do you think I've been doing while I've been waiting for you to get better? I've made you a dress!"

She held up a yellow muslin dress with sprigs of blue flowers and green leaves embroidered onto it.

"It's beautiful!" Lizzie gasped. "Is it really for me?"

"To show off your lovely red hair. I'll leave you to get dressed," Sarah said. "And then we'll go, shall we?"

Lizzie stroked the dress, wondering whether she had ever worn anything as fine and pretty as this before. She knew that hanging in the cupboard in the corner of the room was a plain blue dress. She had often lifted it out secretly and held it against herself. She had seen the girls outside on the track wearing frocks just like these, with white aprons over them. She had watched them, curious, as they hurried along, rapidly tying the apron straps that were ribboning out behind them, fastening the ties of their bonnets. She took the blue frock out of the cupboard now and touched it curiously. *Who did it belong to?* she wondered. *What was it doing there?* It had been torn and mended in several places, and there was a dark stain on the skirt, which looked as if it had been scrubbed at many times. She heard Hetty's heavy step on the landing and guiltily pushed the frock back into the cupboard. *Whatever it is*, she thought, *it can't be anything to do with me.*

"Here, I'll help you into that new frock," Hetty said. "Your arm isn't mended yet, child. Oh, what a lady you look in it! What would your ma think of you?" She turned away quickly, tutting to herself for her thoughtlessness. Hardly any of those apprentice children had mothers any more, and if they did, they had long since been abandoned by them. "Come on now. Be quick. Carriage is waiting."

Lizzie followed her, nervous as a kitten. She had never left the room before, and she glanced round the stairs and the hallway, curious about the dark panelled walls and the heavy furnishings. It was all very different from Sarah's apple-green room. She stepped outside the house and paused to breathe in the warm air; and it was as if she had never breathed it before, never seen trees in full leaf, never heard birds sing.

The carriage was waiting, the door was open, Sarah was inside, smiling at her. And still she stood, gazing round. Hetty bustled ahead with the bags and turned, impatient.

"Come on, lass."

Lizzie hesitated. Something was hauling her back, something was calling, *Wait, wait for me!* Don't go *without me!* But there was no one there, no one to see, no sound except the birds and the incessant sighing of the river.

"Lizzie? Are you ready?"

At last Lizzie nodded, lifted her yellow sprigged skirt, and climbed in next to Sarah.

27

ROBIN'S PLAN

The following Sunday, Emily decided that she would definitely speak to Miss Sarah about Lizzie after the church service. Sunday was a free day; everyone was relaxed. Even sour Master Crispin smiled on a Sunday. She waited nervously outside the church at Oldcastle until the Blackthorn carriage arrived. The pealing bells made her tense and jittery that day, not full of song. She saw the manservant wheel Master Blackthorn down the aisle to the family pew. She saw Mrs Blackthorn following in her crinkly black taffeta dress and her pinched poke bonnet. She saw Master Crispin, smart as a starling, swinging his gold-capped cane. But there was no sign of Miss Sarah. She kept glancing over her shoulder during the hymn singing, listening out for Miss Sarah's voice, but she definitely wasn't there.

When the apprentices came out into sunshine after the service the Blackthorn carriage was already there to take the family home. Emily looked round in despair. If she couldn't ask Miss Sarah, she decided, she would use all her courage and ask her mother.

"I just wish she didn't look so spiky!" she said to Sam, and he squeezed her arm. "Go on! Do it now!" he urged her, and pushed her towards the carriage.

"Mrs Blackthorn! Please, Mrs Blackthorn, may I talk to you?" Sarah called, running behind the family. The mill owner's wife was a little deaf and didn't hear her, and in desperation Sarah had to touch her elbow to make her notice her. Mrs Blackthorn started as though a bee had stung her.

"Was that you?" she asked sharply.

"Please, Mrs Blackthorn, I need to ask you something."

"Me? What on earth can you want to ask me about?"

"Lizzie." Emily took courage from Sam's smiling face on the other side of the carriage lane.

"I don't know any Lizzie," Mrs Blackthorn snorted. "Lizzie who?"

"Lizzie Jarvis. She's my sister."

"Never heard of her." Mrs Blackthorn lifted her

elbow for her son to help her into the carriage. She was clearly annoyed by Emily's boldness. Emily should have dropped back by now, should have run on after the other apprentices, but she clung on to her last hope.

"I brought her to your house when she had an accident," she blurted out.

Master Crispin looked round at her then. "Ah yes, I remember the girl. We had to send for Dr Oxton for her. What happened to her?"

Mrs Blackthorn coloured up. "I told you, Dr Oxton took her away."

"Have you heard nothing since, Mother? If she's better, she should be back at the mill."

"She's dead!" Mrs Blackthorn snapped. She glared round at Emily. "There!"

Emily stood with her hands over her face as the carriage pulled away. She felt numb with horror and pain. Lizzie? Dead? "No, no, she can't be!" she sobbed. "Lizzie. Oh, Lizzie!"

Sam stood awkwardly biting his lip, at her side, wanting to put his arm round her and comfort her.

"She ain't dead, Em'ly. I fink she just said it to shut you up. Didn't you see her face? She was red as a strawberry. She just wanted to get rid of you, I know it."

"Do you really think so, Sam? I'd have heard, wouldn't I? Surely somebody would have told me. Oh, but what if it's true?"

"She can't be dead, she can't be! Mrs Cleggins would have known, wouldn't she?"

"She would have told me," Emily nodded. "She promised she'd tell me if she heard anything at all about Lizzie."

"Mrs Cleggins has a bite like a mad dog sometimes, but she's always fair," Sam said. "She'd never lie to you about your sister."

"She mightn't know though. Oh, Lizzie!" Emily started crying again inside herself in silent, frightened, lonely sorrow.

"Believe me, you'll see her again one day. I know it, Em'ly. Don't give up hope, eh?" Sam walked on beside her, subdued by her silence and despair. He had something to tell her, something important, and he didn't think it could wait. Maybe it would take her mind off Lizzie if he told it now, he thought. He took his chance. "I've got something to tell you. I was going to save it for a bit, but there's a plan, a big plan, to get revenge on that Blackthorn family. They're bad people. Not Miss Sarah, maybe, but all the rest of them. Bad."

Emily hardly listened. She was too dizzy with worry to care what he was saying. She didn't want to talk to him any more. His round white face annoyed her, with his silly permanent grin and his wide innocent eyes. He was soft, that's what everyone said. Soft in the head. Couldn't he see that she wanted to be on her own? She tried to shake him off by striding away from him, head down, but he caught up with her and stood right in front of her, making her stop in her tracks.

"Don't you want to know?" he asked, insistent as a buzzing fly; and when she turned her head away and didn't answer, he added, "Ah, but never mind, because I wasn't going to tell you anyway."

She was still silent.

"Well, I must tell you, because I'm bursting with it! You must promise to keep it a secret. Robin has asked me to do something very special. There, I've told you now. He says I should be very proud to be chosen. He says if I tell anyone he'll cut my throat."

Lizzie looked at him at last, and saw that his

mouth wasn't grinning at all, but was twisted in a tight grimace as though the muscles of his cheeks had clamped up and wouldn't come loose again.

They walked along in silence now, following the line of apprentices back over the hill from Oldcastle. They were both lost in deep thoughts that they could no longer talk about – Emily, with her worry about Lizzie, Sam with his thoughts about Robin and the task he had given him.

"I used to love Sundays," Emily said to herself as they dropped down out of the sunshine into the permanent gloom of Bleakdale. "Now I hate them. Hate them."

She walked on a little ahead of Sam, head down still, in a kind of walking dream all the way down to the valley bottom. When they were on the rough cart track she was startled awake by the sound of trotting hooves coming towards them from the Blackthorn house. The family would be well home by now, so who would be leaving again? Maybe Miss Sarah was in it. This time she would stop it. She had to know the truth about Lizzie. She darted forward with her hand stretched out, but the horses increased their pace and Sam had to grab her elbow and pull her off the track. She put her hands to her face to protect herself from the cloud of dust as the horses swept past.

"I couldn't see! I couldn't see!" she sobbed. "Was Miss Sarah in the carriage?"

"No, she wasn't. It was Master Crispin." He stared after the carriage and let out a long, shuddering sigh. "Tonight's the night then."

Emily turned away at last from the carriage disappearing into the distance. There was no stopping it now. She saw that Sam's face was white and his eyes were haunted with fear. "What do you mean, 'tonight's the night'? Is this something to do with that secret of yours?"

"It's just as Robin said. He heard from someone at the house that Master Crispin will be away tonight. That means, assuming Miss Sarah is away, there's no one there now except the old Master and Mrs Blackthorn. So now's the time to do it."

"To do what?"

Boys were coming towards them now from the apprentice house, calling to each other like homing rooks, arms waving excitedly.

"What he asked me to do. It's revenge. Revenge

against Crick and Master Crispin. It has to be tonight. I'm scared, Em'ly."

He ran away from her towards the lads. In the middle of them all, head and shoulders above the tallest of them, was Robin. Emily remembered Bess's words when they were travelling away from the workhouse in the wagon: "Robin Small, 'e rules us all." He was standing with his hands in his pockets, smiling round fondly at all the boys as though they were his children. From where Emily was standing she could see that he truly had them in his spell; they would do anything for him. He nodded his head towards the mill and all the boys turned to look at it. The shadow of the cold afternoon had fallen on it; the windows were frosty, cold eyes, as if winter had eaten up the summer already. Several boys put up their hands, jostling each other so Robin would see them, but he stepped past them and put his hand on Sam's shoulder. There was a flare of hysterical laughter. Sam shook his head and backed away, and the boys laughed again at something Robin said. Everyone was looking at Sam. And at last he nodded.

The bell was rung for them all to return to the apprentice house for dinner. Some of the boys shook

Sam's hand or slapped him on the shoulder, and then ran off leaving him where he stood with his back to them all, hands deep in his pockets, facing the mill.

When he turned at last to follow them Emily was waiting for him, arms folded. The sun had gone in completely now; the wind had a knife in its hands.

"Sam," she said. "What are they planning? What has Robin asked you to do?"

Sam started, not seeing her at first, he was so lost in his thoughts. "What? What do you mean?"

"You and those other boys. You're not doing anything to harm the mill, are you?"

Sam shrugged, trying to push past her.

"You're such a fool, Sam Jenkins, if you do what that Robin tells you to do. It's all right for him to think up his big evil plans and then to order you to carry them out. He won't be doing anything himself, will he? He'd see you swing for it, whatever it is, and he'd get away, smirking his silly head off. Tell me what the plan is."

"I can't." He was as miserable as a wet cat.

"I'll never speak to you again if you don't."

Sam bent down, picked up a loose stone from the track and hurled it into the river. She couldn't see his face, only hear the twisted agony in his voice.

"I don't want to do it. He's forced me. He's picked some of us to do the job, and if we don't do it, he's going to tell Crick we had a plan against him and Master Crispin. He said he'll kill me, Em'ly, if I don't do it. I'm the main one. He'll kill me if I don't do it."

28

THE SHEEN

Lizzie was asleep, but was gently wakened by Sarah shaking her shoulder. She was in a daze still when she stepped out of the carriage and looked around at the fine red-brick house, the slope of green lawn and the flowerbeds frothing with colour. White seagulls cruised overhead, making heart-rending calls as if they were longing for something they could never have; home, maybe, or a safe resting place. There was a fresh, strong, salty smell, and a long, whispering sigh. *Shee-sheee-shee* it went. It came from beyond the gardens, and Lizzie could see a strip of blue, endless, shimmering, restless blue, flecked here and there with glances of white.

"That's the sea!" Sarah laughed. "Isn't it wonderful, Lizzie! Welcome, welcome to my favourite place in the world!"

In the grand red house with its huge windows that looked out to the sea, Lizzie met Sarah's Aunt

Gillian. She was small and grey-haired and had a puckering mischievous smile that sometimes made her look very young. She told Lizzie that she was very pretty, and most welcome, gave her some cake and took her up to a room that was almost as blue as the sea itself.

"It will be dark soon, so it's nearly bedtime. Would you like to sleep now?" she asked.

Lizzie nodded. She was still dazed from the journey and confused about where she was and why she was there, but she didn't want to have to talk to anyone – not yet. Miss Gillian smiled and left the room, and Lizzie paced round it like a cat, frightened to touch anything, and didn't relax until Hetty came in with some night-clothes for her.

"This sea air will be nice for you," Hetty said, opening the windows wide. "I like to listen to the waves. Would you like to hear it? It'll rock you to sleep better than any lullaby. You'll sleep well tonight, I promise you that. I've got some errands to do now but you might see Eglantine in a bit." She stood with her arms folded, gazing at the sea, then turned round to look at Lizzie. "I'm glad Miss Sarah's brought you here."

"So am I," Lizzie faltered. "But I feel strange, Hetty. I don't know why I've come, or whether I'm going back. I don't know anything, and it's so strange." She felt the sting of tears in her eyes and a sob rising in her voice. She couldn't help it. "What's happening?"

"I don't know what Miss Sarah has in mind, except to get you well again, so make the most of it, Lizzie child. I suppose I should call you Miss Lizzie, but I can't get it right in my head. I don't know what's going to happen to you, and that's the truth." She took Lizzie's hands in both her own and squeezed them, tight. "You cry if you want. It always makes me feel better, a good cry."

She lifted her apron to her face and dabbed her own eyes with it, and left. Lizzie was alone again. The air grew cold, and she struggled to close the window and draw the curtains against the darkening sky. There were no houses to be seen, no hill, no trees. There was nothing out there but gleaming sand; nothing but early stars in the deep dark sky; nothing for miles and miles.

Before long an elderly maid with blotchy skin and trembling hands brought a tray of food. She dithered in the doorway for a bit, peering round the room, and then lurched forward towards Lizzie.

"Are you Eglantine?" Lizzie asked.

"I am, Miss Elzibeth. Miss Gillian thought you might like to eat this up here but if you want to join them in the dining room you can only you might have to carry the tray yourself cos I can do coming upstairs all right but I don't do downstairs easy these days with these knees so your Hetty will bring it down in the morning." She slid her lips apart in a smile that showed very few teeth. Everything on the tray rattled. Lizzie closed her eyes, letting a wisp of memory drift across her mind like smoke. It floated away before she could make sense of it.

"I'd like to eat it in here. Thank you."

Eglantine sucked her gums and set the tray down on a table near the window. "Very sensible nice lamb chops can't eat them any more not in public pick them up in my fingers but not very polite nice mashed potatoes and peas only some rolled off the plate on the carpet too look I've squashed them with my foot that's bad so there you are need feeding up you do." She peered again at Lizzie. "Friend of Miss Sarah's or some relative I don't know but I been here since her mother was born so I'd know you if you was."

"I think I'm a kind of friend," said Lizzie, frowning, and the maid slid her mouth open again and rattled with laughter.

"Miss Elzibeth you're a funny one you are you say words funny don't you? I'll light the lamp now and if you want a fire lit someone else can do it I can't with my knees it's the bending you see not good eat it all up now there's a good girl. Good night."

Lizzie woke up to the keening of seagulls. They sobbed as if their hearts would break, as if they were lost souls who would never find their loved ones again. She ran to the windows and pulled back the curtains, and there it was – the sea, the bright sheen of it, the immense blue spread of it. She watched the rolling waves of the incoming tide, and the way the foam raced across the sand as though someone had flung a lacy veil out, and dragged it back, and swirled it out again. It was mesmerising; she couldn't take her eyes off it. She didn't even hear the door to her room opening and someone coming to stand behind her.

"Isn't it beautiful?" said Miss Sarah. "We'll walk down to it after breakfast. Or would you like to go now?"

"Oh now, please now!" Lizzie begged.

Sarah laughed. "I'm pleased you said that. After breakfast the tide will have gone out and the sand will be soggy to walk in. High tide is the best time. It's such a shame to miss it."

"Won't it come back?" Lizzie asked anxiously.

"Oh yes, the tide comes back. It takes about twelve hours, but it will come back. But it goes a very long way, so far that all you can see is a thin line of the dark horizon between the sky and the sand. And that's beautiful too. Miles and miles of sand. Get your warm cloak. The air is still fresh at this time of the morning. Then we'll run down and say hello to the sea."

The beach was just at the bottom of the garden. They went down through the gate, followed by the two joyous dogs that belonged to Sarah's Aunt Gillian, and ploughed down the golden slope of sand that led down towards the level shore. Lizzie was excited by the sound of the sea and the seabirds. She ran straight to the edge of the waves, then backed away in alarm as the water streamed out towards her, lapping round her new boots. Sarah laughed.

"It's like a hungry beast! It's chasing you! But it won't come any higher now. It's just on the turn, I think. See where our feet have sunk into the damp sand behind us? It's been up as far as that, and left a little trail of seaweed behind. The wading birds will come soon in case the sea has left them any breakfast."

She perched herself on a boulder and patted it for Lizzie to come and sit next to her. Lizzie felt safe there, secure and warm in her cloak, pressed against Sarah's side. They sat together quietly, listening to the suck and pull of the waves and the keening of the white gulls as they circled overhead.

"I could sit here for hours and watch the sea," Sarah murmured. "I miss it so much when I'm in Bleakdale. I wish I didn't have to go back there, ever." But she was speaking to herself, almost as if she had forgotten that Lizzie was there. There was such longing in her voice. "This is my home, really. This is where I really want to be."

Lizzie glanced up at her. She wanted to say:

I don't know what home is. I don't know where I belong. Sarah seemed to remember then that Lizzie was there, and she pointed over to where a tongue of land stretched across the horizon.

"Over there, it's another country," she said. "It's called Wales. You can see the mountains."

"Mountains? What are they?" Lizzie asked timidly.

"Well, they're very high hills. Much higher than the hills of Bleakdale even. And over in the other direction is Liverpool. Have you heard of Liverpool? No? I'll take you there one day. We'll see the big ships coming in with all their cargoes of cotton for the mills. They've come all the way from America. Have you heard of America?"

Again Lizzie shook her head. She bit her lip, ashamed. "I don't know about any of these things. I don't know anything."

"Well, you do now, because I've told you!" Sarah smiled down at her. "Don't be upset, Lizzie. It's not your fault. Nobody knows these things until they're told about them. That's what education is. After breakfast I can show you these places on a map. Would you like that?"

"Yes please, Miss Sarah," said Lizzie, though she had no idea what a map was.

Sarah stood up and clapped her hands together. "We'll do it, Lizzie! This is how we'll spend our time here, while you're getting better. I'll be your teacher! We'll walk by the sea every day and that will make you strong and well again, and we'll have lessons afterwards. I don't want you to call me Miss Sarah, by the way."

"Hetty does," said Lizzie doubtfully.

"But Hetty's a servant. Now you chase the dogs as far as the jetty there, to get some roses in your cheeks and give you an appetite. Eglantine will be getting breakfast ready now. You've met Eglantine, I suppose? Crispin and I used to call her Stop-for-breath, because she never did. Off you go!"

It was hard work running in sand. Lizzie felt as if she had weights tied to her feet, and she had to keep her skirts bunched up and take long strides to keep her balance. It made her laugh out loud; and she couldn't remember when she had last laughed. When she reached the jetty she turned round, waving triumphantly. Sarah was standing where she had left her, still gazing out to sea. Lizzie watched her, biting her lip.

Who is she? she wondered. *And who am I? If I'm not a servant, I don't know who I am.*

29

REVENGE

Emily had no idea what to do next. Surely Sam hadn't mean what he had told her – kind, gentle, smiling Sam? Would he really do anything to damage the mill? Surely he would find a way of telling Mrs Cleggins or somebody what Robin was planning, whatever it was? And yet she had seen the fear in his eyes and heard it in his voice. He was afraid of Robin Small. And so was she, now. She was afraid for Sam. She decided that she must tell Mrs Cleggins that there were plans to damage the mill. Mrs Cleggins might shout at her and clack her teeth at her, might slap her cheek for bothering her when she was busy; or she might listen quietly to what she said. It all depended on what mood she was in. But she had to know, and she was probably the only person who could help.

Mrs Cleggins was in her room. Emily paced up and down outside the door, waiting for her to come out. When she didn't she screwed up her courage and knocked. The house mistress yanked the door open and glowered at her. She was in one of her fiercest moods that day. She wouldn't listen when Emily asked if she could speak to her. She said she had a headache like someone beating a tin drum, and she couldn't be doing with anyone mithering her.

"Leave me be. You've to do your own schooling today," she announced. "Skivvy's already put your food out. I'll see you at bedtime if I'm not dead by then." She slammed her door shut behind her and refused to answer it.

There was no sign of Skivvy; no one at all for Emily to speak to. Sam kept himself away from Emily, ate his food with his head down, drew on his slate without glancing her way. He always had a group of boys around him; he always had Robin watching him. Emily was desperate to speak to him again now, to find out as much as she could, and at last she saw him leaving the apprentice house on his own. She slipped out after him. He was walking very slowly, hands deep in his pockets, and Emily soon caught up with him.

"What's happening? Go on, tell me."

Sam couldn't speak for wretchedness and shame.

"It's something you've got to do tonight, while Master Crispin is away, right?" she prompted. "Before he gets back and stops you doing it?"

Sam broke down then. He stood with his hands covering his face, blubbering into them like a small, frightened child. She couldn't hear what he was saying; she had to pull his hands away from his face and make him repeat it.

"He wants us to set fire to the mill. He wants us to burn it down. And he's chosen me to light the torch."

Emily shook him by his shoulders. She wanted him to deny what he had just told her, she wanted to push it out of her mind and think about Lizzie instead, but she couldn't. She had seen fires in London, long ago when she was a little girl. She had seen whole houses burning down as if they were made of paper, roofs and walls gaping open like terrified mouths. She remembered the waves of black smoke; the red, impossible anger of flames, the screams of people trapped inside the buildings. She remembered what Skivvy had said about Buxford Mill; nearly all the girls on the top floors had perished. Mrs Cleggins's husband had burnt to death.

"When?"

"Tonight, Em'ly. Robin's sent me now to hide behind the mill till it's properly dark. The other chosen ones will come one by one, and someone will hand me the torch. I'm to be the one to set it alight."

"It can't be true! It can't! You mustn't do it. You mustn't let it happen!"

"I can't stop it," he moaned. "It's Robin's plan, not mine. He says it's for all of us, it's revenge for all the misery and all the dying."

"It's the wrong way to do it. Think of the bales of cotton, the wooden machines, the bobbins and looms and spinning machines! They'd burn down in seconds. Think of the people, Sam, trapped upstairs, right up to the top of the building! How would they get out? They'd burn to death! Is that what you want?"

"It's Sunday. There won't be no people there today."

"There'll be girls cleaning the machines. There'll be people mending stuff. Some people sleep up there, you know they do. The carriers from Liverpool sometimes. Old skivvies who can't walk up and down the hill any more."

"I don't know, I don't know!" Sam was sobbing now, his knuckles pressed against his ears as if he wanted to muffle and drown every word Emily was saying. "What can I do?"

"You can speak to Master Blackthorn, that's what."

"I daren't tell Master!" Sam moaned. "Robin will find out and get me killed for it. He'll see me there; he'll know."

"Then get yourself up the hill and over to Oldcastle. Try and get some help from someone. You must tell the workers to come and stop it happening."

She shoved him away from her and he plunged down the path and lumbered up the steep track that led over the hill to Oldcastle. He was sobbing loudly now. Emily turned one way and another, not knowing for sure what she should do next. Maybe she should follow Sam, help him to spread the word more quickly. But the owner of the mill should know first, surely. She would have to tell Master Blackthorn herself; and what could he do, a sick old man in a wheelchair? Maybe the house servants would come and help her. Help her to do what? Fight off Robin's gang of thugs? And where were they now, creeping in the gloomy afternoon like cunning foxes. Dusk was already gathering; shadows lengthening. Had they heard her and Sam? She ran towards the mill house and hammered at the door with both fists, terrified in case Robin's watchers were following her, ready to pounce on her any minute and drag her away, ready to beat her.

There was no answer at the main door. She turned and ran to the window, standing on tiptoe to try to peer in and attract someone's attention, but she wasn't tall enough. She looked upwards at the darkening hillside. She could just make out the dim shape of Sam bobbing up the footpath like a skittering rabbit. "Go quickly, Sam! Be speedy," she whispered. And then she saw him veer off the path and away towards a copse of woods. Very soon he disappeared from sight. "What on earth is he doing?" she asked herself. "That's not the way to Oldcastle!" But she knew very well what he was doing. He had deserted her. He had taken fright, and he had gone into hiding in the woods.

She went round into the cobbled courtyard and to the door of the servants' quarters, drumming on it, kicking it, trying to force it open. Were they all asleep in there? At last the door was opened by a yawning maid. Emily pushed past her and into the house.

"What do you think you're doing?" the maid shrieked.

"I must see Master Blackthorn, I must!" Emily shouted.

"You can't! He's having his supper!" the maid shouted back. "Get away with you, this minute."

"Master Blackthorn!" Emily shouted, as the maid tried to hustle her back out of the door. "Master Blackthorn!" She ran through the kitchen, up the stairs and into the hallway, dithering because she had no idea then where to go next. "Danger!"

Master Blackthorn heard the commotion, and signalled to Fergus to wheel him to where Emily was standing. His wife followed, dabbing her lips with her napkin.

"That girl again!" she gasped. "Throw her out, Fergus. Heave-ho with her!"

Emily bent to the wheelchair and clutched Master Blackthorn's mottled hand. "Master Blackthorn, please come! You must. Some of the apprentices are going to burn down the mill."

"My mill? My mill?"

"Tonight, sir."

Master Blackthorn could tell by her face and her voice that she wasn't lying. He banged his hands on the sides of his chair with a roar of rage. "Wheel me down there, Fergus. Send someone for Crispin."

"There's no one," his wife snapped. "He's taken the carriage. We have only ourselves, the servants and that silly new girl in the house. We can't do anything against a mob of apprentices."

"Take me to the apprentice house," Master Blackthorn ordered Fergus. "I'll speak to them myself."

Emily followed them out of the house and ran behind them to the apprentice house, where she knew that all the children except Sam would be sitting down at the tables, ready for the meal. Skivvy would be serving out the bowls of porridge; Mrs Cleggins would be having her own meal in peace.

Mrs Blackthorn was marching ahead of them, fury and fear in her stride. She had never been inside the apprentice house before. She would face a mob of angry hooligans, she knew it. She remembered the gangs that had attacked the mill years ago when the first lot of new machinery had been bought. She remembered how they attacked her husband, beat him, forced him to the ground and broke his back. She would defend him now, for sure. These wild ruffians would be defeated, if she had to do it on her own. She thrust open the door and stood waiting for the uproar. She took in the grey, thin faces of the children, the slops they were being served for their meal, the cold, dim room that was their home. Not a mob at all, but a roomful of silent, frightened children. She turned away, ashamed, and let her husband speak.

"Is this true? Is this true?" he shouted. "This girl tells me you are planning to sabotage my mill? Is this true, boy?" he yelled at the closest child, little Alfie. He shook his head and covered his face with his hands, too afraid to speak.

"You, is it true?" he pointed at one of the older boys sitting next to Robin. The boy, flustered, turned to look at Robin, who stood up slowly, looking deeply concerned.

"I hope not, Master Blackthorn," he said. "But you should know that one of the boys is missing." He cast a smile towards Emily, hovering in the doorway, and sat down again.

Emily shook her head, dumb with fright. Should she run after Sam and warn him? She started to back away, then realised that it was not just Sam who was missing. There were several empty places, here and there, gaps in the benches where the older boys always sat. "Master Blackthorn –" she began, but he swung round in his chair.

"Silence!" he roared. "You have said enough for now."

Mrs Cleggins came running from her room, wiping her mouth with her apron. She stopped in alarm when she saw the mill owner and his wife in the apprentice room. To her knowledge neither of them had ever been inside it before.

"Mistress Cleggins," Master Blackthorn's voice was choking in his throat now. His wife put a hand on his shoulder. "You are responsible for these apprentice workers! If what this girl says is true, then one of them is planning to set fire to my mill."

"Never!" she said. "Oh, Mester Blackthorn, I've never heard any talk of that."

"Do you know how serious this could be, if it is

true?" He motioned to Fergus to wheel him up and down the room, so he could rap every table with his fist as he passed it. "Do you know that all our profit will be lost, that all the cotton, all the machinery, everything would catch fire in seconds? My mill would go. Bleakdale Mill would be lost for ever. If such a thing should happen, every one of you would be responsible, not just the missing boy."

Mrs Cleggins looked wildly round the room, counting heads. "Who? Who's missing?" she moaned.

Emily stepped away from the apprentice room. Unnoticed, she slipped into the protection of the darkness. There was no interrupting Master Blackthorn now. Besides, they might be too late already. The other boys might be hiding in those dense shrubs near the mill, waiting to find Sam and hand him the tinder that would light his brushwood torch. And if he wasn't there, would they still do it themselves? She turned and ran towards the mill itself. The gates were unlocked. She burst through them and raced into the dark building and up the steps, shouting "Anyone there? Anyone there?" She could hear scuffling. Rats perhaps, foraging into the cotton bales. Machines being cleaned and prepared for the next day. Old tired workers who hid in the dark corners at night. Maybe their own Skivvy, sleeping off her Sunday chores. Or Robin's followers, already on the prowl? "Get out! Get out!" she shouted, and her voice echoed round the vast lonely building. "Fire! Fire! Get out!"

An old man, bent-backed and hollow-eyed, shuffled out from a behind a pile of cotton bales. "Fire?" he croaked. "Where, lass? I don't see none."

"There might be. Tell the others. Tell everyone who's here," Emily begged him. "Get everyone out of the building. Especially from the top floors. I'm going to get help."

He stared at her vacantly, mouth dropping open.

"Just do it!" Emily moaned. "Just warn them."

She ran out of the mill, kicked off her clogs and hurried on up the stony track towards Oldcastle. Her feet were bleeding and sore, her legs ached from trying to run uphill. "Soon, soon, I'll meet someone," she told herself. "Soon I'll find help." The wind was squalling now, flinging cold rain into her face. The moon was full up but hiding in rain clouds, and she had no lantern with her. She paused to take her breath, almost too tired to carry on. She turned her head away from the rain and faced Bleakdale.

Far below her, in the dark valley, a light flared.

"It's the torch!" she groaned. "They're going to do it. I'm too late."

She sank down onto a boulder, much too tired now to carry on. She watched in fascinated horror as a huge flame spiralled up as if it was trying to eat the sky. It seemed to happen in seconds. The light of flames pressed against every window, the burning tongue licked its way out of the roof. She could see the silhouette of the mill with its hundreds of red and angry eyes. There was nothing she could do now. She would wait there, and wait there, and she would see the building crouching down to the ground like a sleeping monster.

But now she could hear a clamour of voices carried up to her on the wind. She could see small black shapes moving, shadows against the flaming light, lanterns bobbing. Maybe they were coming to help to put out the fire. She began to move slowly down the hill, hardly daring to hope, then she scrambled faster and faster. She began to run, not caring any more about her wounded feet, gulping in air. She saw the lights of a carriage swaying down the valley road track. People were clambering out of it. Then a wagon came, and another. Now she could make out more lanterns. There were chains of people stretching up from the river to the mill, passing pails to one another. As she reached the bottom track she could smell choking, acid smoke; she could hear people coughing and retching. She worked her way to the building and saw that Master Blackthorn himself was at the very front of the chain in his wheelchair, flinging bucket after bucket of water into the mill. Now another wagon had arrived, and there were firemen leaping from it. How had they come so quickly? she wondered. Where had all these people come from? Now a man was jumping down from another carriage. She could hear him barking orders, pushing himself through the crowd to the front, flinging off his coat to reveal a flash of yellow in the light of the lanterns. Surely that was Master Crispin? How had he found out about the fire when he was away from home? But there was no time to think about that. She rushed to help where she could, joining onto the chain of sweating villagers and apprentices.

Now the firemen were stretching a hose from the river, plumes of water were jetting and hissing, fountaining over everyone and everything near the burning mill. And the flame, the tongue of destruction, was falling back, back down into the throat of the building. The fire was surely dying down.

Another carriage arrived, bells clanging, lights swinging. Police officers jumped out, shouting, swinging sticks, which they used to thump anyone who got in their way. Master Crispin left the line of water bearers and led the policemen to a scuffle of figures on the ground. Some of the older apprentice boys were twisting and writhing, held down by hefty overseers. Mrs Cleggins was holding a lantern high above them, kicking anyone who rolled anywhere near her.

"You've let me down, lads. Let me down!" she shrieked. The policemen trussed the boys up as if they were chickens to be taken to the market, and bundled them into the police wagons. Emily scanned the faces of the lads as the wagon trundled away. There was no sign of Sam among them. She saw a figure slipping into the shadows at the side of the mill and ran forwards, thinking for a moment that it might be Sam. But the figure was too tall, and didn't limp like Sam did these days.

She was almost certain it was Robin, slipping away like a wily fox into the night.

30

I CAN'T REMEMBER

After breakfast with Aunt Gillian, Sarah took Lizzie into the room she called the library. The walls were lined with glass cases, and inside them were shelves of leather-bound books: green, black, brown, red, all with gold lettering on the spines. Sarah took down one of the larger books and opened it out on the table. "This is the atlas. I'll show you the map of England first. It's a funny shape, isn't it? Like a begging dog. There's London. That's the capital."

"London," Lizzie repeated.

Sarah watched her keenly. She knew by the way Lizzie spoke that she would have come from London, but the child showed no recognition of the word. "That's its big river, the Thames." Still nothing. "And right up here, this is Liverpool. Remember we could just see it this morning?"

"L-iv-er-pool. Is that what it says? The big ships bring cotton there, from America."

"Well done! Look, here's Manchester, and on the other side of the hills, there's Sheffield. And these hills are called the Pennines. They stretch right up from there to the north of the country. And this" – she pointed to an unnamed spot on the map – "this is where we came from yesterday. This is where my father's mill is."

Lizzie frowned. Her finger traced the route.

"What's cotton?" she asked suddenly. "Why does it come to Liverpool? Where's America?"

Sarah sat down. "Can you read and write, Lizzie?"

Lizzie shook her head, frowning. "I don't think so."

"I think you know some of the letters, but you've forgotten. I'm going to give them back to you. It's the most important thing you can learn, to read and write. And I'd like to be the one to teach you."

Lizzie stared at her, mystified. Why was it so important, so special? she wondered. Could everyone do it?

Sarah brought some paper, some ink, and two quill pens. She spread them out on the table. "You'll have done some letters already at the apprentice school?"

Lizzie couldn't remember. She had no idea what Sarah meant by the apprentice school. There was that fog again in her mind when she tried to think about it, and an inexplicable memory of sadness and loss. Familiar tears scorched her eyes.

"I'll write out letters for you to copy. And by lunchtime, I promise, you'll be able to write your own name. Lizzie…?"

"Yes. Lizzie."

"I know. But what comes next? I'm Sarah Blackthorn. You're Lizzie…?"

Now the tears brimmed over and coursed down her cheeks, unstoppable. "I don't know. I don't know if I've got another name. I can't remember."

Lizzie was in the library, working by herself. She had been living in Aunt Gillian's house for a week, having lessons every day, and she could copy whole pages by now. She was drawing a map of England, filling in the names of the major towns, saying them out loud to herself as she wrote them down.

Sarah and Aunt Gillian were sitting in the sunny morning room looking out over the sand. The tide was out; the sea was miles away. In the distance the long line of indigo horizon was flecked with the shapes of steamships bringing their cargoes of cotton, spices and fruit from all over the world towards the bay of Liverpool.

Aunt Gillian watched her niece. Something was on her mind, she could tell that. She stood up suddenly and started prowling up and down the room like a restless cat searching for a warm place to settle.

"Are you thinking about the child?" she asked Sarah carefully.

"Yes. I am."

"So what are your plans for her, Sarah?"

"I have no real plans. I want to make her well again. I want to make her happy, after the terrible injuries she received at our mill. I suppose I feel responsible, in a way."

"Don't be ridiculous! How could you be responsible?"

"I saw the conditions those children work in – all that dangerous machinery with no guards to protect them, all that cotton stuff floating round them, so they can only breathe it in. Some of the overlookers are really cruel too, beating them to get as much work as possible out of them. I saw it all, and I did nothing to help them. Now's my chance, Aunt Gillian. I can't help them all. But I can help one child."

"And when she's better? What then? Are you going to send her back to the same miserable conditions?"

Sarah went to stand by the window. "How can I? She nearly died there!" She paused, shy to tell her aunt about her secret wish. "The fact is, I think I want to give her a home. Permanently. With me. I'd like her to think of me as her sister."

Lizzie had just at that moment come into the room to show Sarah the map she had drawn. She stopped in the doorway, hand pressed to her mouth. Had she heard that word right? Sister? Sister? The word shocked her. It had strong, emotional, hurtful associations. She backed away and ran from the morning room and straight down to the kitchen where Eglantine and Hetty were preparing dinner. Eglantine was plucking a chicken. Lizzie flung herself into Hetty's arms.

"Child, child, whatever's the matter?" Hetty asked her.

"She's heartbroke she is and no one can help her only Miss Sarah she's got a kind heart she has not like her brother in that dark place I don't wonder this child's crying." Eglantine flumped the chicken on the table to shake the loose feathers off.

But Lizzie couldn't find the words to explain her confusion at the sound of the word "sister". It had opened up a hole in her memory, like a door swinging free for a second, and then it had slammed shut again. "I don't know who I am," she managed to sob, but that wasn't it, that wasn't the half of it.

"I don't know either," Hetty said. "I know what happened to you and why you was brought to the house, but Miss Sarah made me promise not to talk to you about it because it might stop you getting better. I daren't tell you. She says she wants your good memories to come back first. And they will. They will." She released Lizzie from her arms. "I'm about to take their morning tea through to them. You can help me set tray, if you like."

"I've got good and bad memories my first is I can remember throwing flour all over my brother," Eglantine said dreamily. "He looked like a ghosty I can't say I like him much but I think about him every time I put my hands in a sack of flour."

Hetty had learnt the art of not listening to a word

Eglantine was saying, Instead of replying, she was watching in surprise as Lizzie moved confidently round the kitchen. "Well, lass, you've set that tray nicely. Anyone would think you'd done it before."

Lizzie stepped back and surveyed the tray, strangely pleased with herself: cups, saucers, teaspoons, sugar, milk, plates, teapot. "Do they want biscuits?"

"Miss Gillian likes scones," said Eglantine. "Miss Sarah doesn't but two for Miss Gillian and a spot of jam with them in the pot on the shelf good oh my back's killing me today."

Lizzie stared at her, then turned away. "May I take the tray up to them?" she asked.

"If you want to," Hetty laughed. "I think they'll have a nice surprise if you do. Don't drop it, mind. Here, I shall bring teapot. I don't want you scalding yourself."

Lizzie let Hetty go ahead of her. She lifted the tray carefully, balancing the weight. As she carried it out of the kitchen and up the stairs memories flittered like summer butterflies. Two old ladies sitting bolt upright in a bed; a girl with a face like a moon of white dough; someone...someone kind; a woman with plump arms; the smell of bread baking in an oven.

Hetty had left the morning room door open and Lizzie walked in slowly, set the tray down in front of Sarah, and poured out the tea. Her hands were shaking. Hetty nodded to her and left the room.

"What a lovely surprise!" said Sarah, smiling at Lizzie. "Come and sit with us."

Lizzie shook her head. She put her hands on the edge of the table to steady herself. There was something she had to do, words she had to say.

"Please tell me. I want to know what happened to me."

Much later, Lizzie went out of the house and down to the beach. The tide was nudging back in; she could see the white curl of foam far away, she could hear the distant thunder of the waves, and the plangent cry of gulls.

She knew now that she was an apprentice. That she had worked in the mill that belonged to Sarah's father. She knew that her scavenging job meant scrambling under heavy moving machinery every day to gather up cotton fluff and dust. She also knew that she had nearly been suffocated when the straps of her apron caught in the machine and squeezed tighter and tighter around her. She knew that a girl had put her in a kind of wheelbarrow and trundled her to the mill house, and that Hetty and Sarah had nursed her back to life. Hetty had told her then that the girl from the mill had come to the house to ask how she was, and that was how they knew her name was Lizzie.

She picked up a pebble and nursed it in her palm, then knelt down and drew her name with it in the damp sand. LIZZIE. "That's me," she said. "And the tide will come in and wash my name away, and no one will ever know, till I write it again." She knew that Sarah would be standing watching her from the window, guarding her, loving her.

The ache inside herself was like a yawning hollow, it was like the cave that a huge wave held inside itself, rearing up, rearing up, time after time after time. She flung the pebble as far as she could and turned back to the house.

31

AFTER THE FIRE

In the apprentice house, in the days after the fire, the children watched each other listlessly, horrified by what they had seen. Every day they helped to clean up the mess the fire had made, dragging out the charred remains of cotton bales and bundling them on carts to be carried away, baling out water, mopping and sponging, till their backs ached and their clothes were damp rags. The machines lay like broken, blackened limbs. Men hauled them out of the building and made a pile like a charnel-heap in the mill yard. Some of the downstairs windows had exploded, and the glass had to be cleared away and the holes boarded up. But the charred walls stayed upright, the roof and the top floor were firm. The police came and questioned all the apprentices to find out what they knew, and they all spoke the truth. They were too frightened to do otherwise. Robin Small was behind it, and

Robin Small had disappeared. So had Sam.

At the end of the week, Mr Blackthorn called everyone to a meeting. They all came together, apprentices and the older workers and children from over the hill in Oldcastle. They all trooped into the mill and stood huddled together, shivering in its damp silence. Emily stood with Miriam, remembering that terrible moment when Master Blackthorn had ordered Fergus to wheel him to the apprentice house, how he had been rolled up and down the aisles, rapping his hand on the tables, his eyes glaring and angry. She remembered how Robin had stood up and told him about the missing boy, Sam. And then she remembered how she had run away from the house. Surely, surely, she and Sam were going to be blamed now. And where was Sam anyway? She saw how frail Mr Blackthorn was looking now, his square face almost grey with fatigue, his hair white and matted. He was hunched up in his chair like a cornered spider. It was as if all the spirit had gone out of him, all the passion for Bleakdale Mill evaporated. In a week he had turned into an old man. But Master Crispin stayed firm beside him, his hand on his father's shoulder.

"Here we go," Miriam whispered. "We're in for a right old telling-off now."

"Quiet, everyone!" Master Crispin roared. A frightened hush fell across the crowd. "My father's got words for you all about the mill."

"I have indeed," Master Blackthorn began. "I want to thank you for saving our mill. We would never have managed without you."

Master Crispin looked down at him, surprised. He hadn't been expecting this, it was obvious to see. There was a grunt of approval from the mill workers. Miriam glanced at Emily and raised her eyebrows.

"The mill has been saved, by your efforts," Master Blackthorn went on. "And many lives have been spared. There was but one casualty. One of the overseers lost his life when a burnt spar fell on him. That was Nathaniel Crick. He died in hospital."

There was a moment's aghast silence. Miriam clutched Emily's hand and squeezed it tight. Crick; vindictive, cruel, snarling Crick. He had haunted many a worker's nightmares. "I have no pity for him," she whispered. "I know it's wicked to say it, but I haven't." Emily stared at her, horrified to hear her giving voice to such thoughts.

"As my father said," Master Crispin added, "Bleakdale Mill is saved. But it will be some time before it can be put to use again. Months. We have to have some of the floors, stairs, windows, doors replaced. Most of all we need new machinery."

His father lifted his hand to stop him. *It's my mill*, his look said. *This is my speech.* "All the new machinery will be safe, with proper guards on all the moving parts." His voice was weak and rumbling, but everybody heard it, everyone noticed the surprised look on Master Crispin's face, as if this was something they had never discussed.

Emily bent her head. *Too late*, she thought. *Too late for Lizzie. Too late for all the maimed workers here, all the people who've lost arms and hands to the machines.* She thought of Crick and the missing fingers of his right hand. Was that why he was so cruel? she wondered. Was that why he hated everyone so much?

"We will employ the men and the older boys among you to help with the building work and joinery," The mill owner continued. "As for the rest of you – we would hope to employ you again in the future, but we can't pay you anything till then.

There may be some work over at Cressdale Mill for those who can get that far, and I'll arrange for the mill owner there to release you when the time comes to open up Bleakdale again." There was a tremor in his voice. "I want you all to come back and work for me."

"The apprentices are no longer needed," Master Crispin added abruptly. "They are released from their contract and will be returned to the workhouse today. The wagons are on their way now."

The meeting was over. The dismissed workers moved away, muttering. Some of the women were crying, mopping their faces with their shawls and aprons. Some of the younger men were slapping each other on the back, shaking hands, pleased to know that they'd be given jobs with the building work. "He's been fair," they said to each other. "That's what I've always thought about Master Blackthorn. He's strict but he's fair."

"Master Crispin thinks mill's his already, but it ain't, not yet. The old man as good as told him that today," one of the spinners said.

The apprentices turned to one another, not knowing at first what to make of the news that they had all been dismissed for good. "So, back to the workhouse, after all that!" Miriam said. "Can't say I'll be sorry to leave this gloomy hole. Will you?"

Emily shook her head. She didn't know what to think. She had no home to go to now, but she'd never even been to the workhouse. Would they take her in? She hated the thought of it; everything that Ma and Rosie had ever told her about the workhouse made her cold with dread. But maybe Jim was there. Maybe she would see him again. She hadn't seen him for well over a year. Yet how could she leave Bleakdale, not knowing what had happened to Lizzie? *I won't leave you behind*; that had been her promise. What if she really was dead? She couldn't bear to think about it. What if her body lay in an unmarked grave in that patch of earth over the river, along with Bess and the other lost children? She had to find out for sure before she could ever bring herself to leave the valley.

And where was Sam, kind, simple Sam; her best friend? Would she ever see him again? Had he been caught by Robin?

By the time they got back to the house, most of the apprentices were excited about leaving Bleakdale.

They thronged together, cheerfully sorting out their old clothes from the chest where they had been kept by Skivvy, throwing them out to each other as if they were pulling a nest to pieces. Mrs Cleggins watched them in silence, making no attempt to keep them in order. Now the apprentices were leaving she had no job, and no home to go to. They chattered around her like excited starlings.

"This don't fit me no more!" Miriam said, holding her dress against herself, and she half smiled, remembering how Robin had paid her a compliment all those months ago. "I wonder what happened to him?" she said.

Everyone knew who she was talking about. "'E's either swinging from a scaffold or 'e's the new Lord Mayor of London," somebody said.

"I hope I never sees him again, is all," said little Alfie, shuddering. "It was all his idea, this was."

"Ah, I do," sighed Miriam. "I know what he did was wrong, the way he did it, and forced the lads to do his dirty work for him an' all, but think – it gets us away from here, and it gets safe machinery for the new mill. He did some good, even if he didn't mean to!"

"I wouldn't want to work at the new mill though, safe or not. I've had enough of this place, I have," said Dulcie. "Wagons'll be here soon, and we'll never see sunny Bleakdale again. Back to Mr Sissons and the others at the workhouse. Charming, they were. I bet they've missed us, good and proper. Pining for us, they've been!"

Amid the clatter of laughter Emily sat staring in front of her. Miriam handed her Lizzie's rag doll and she held it pressed to her chest, hugged inside her folded-up arms. *I won't let anyone take this away from me*, she thought. *It's all I've got of Lizzie.*

At last Mrs Cleggins roused herself and shooed them all out to wait for the wagons. Emily looked round, realising that she was alone in the room now, and stood up hesitantly. How bare it seemed without the other children. How bleak and sunless. She remembered where Lizzie and Bess used to sit, huddled up together, sharing secrets; she remembered how jealous she had been of their closeness. As she stood there in a sad kind of waking dream, one of the boys put his head round the door. "Em'ly, go down behind the millrace," he whispered. "There's a someone there as wants to see you."

"Lizzie!" Emily pushed him aside and ran out of the schoolroom, past all the apprentice children who were hopping about, impatient and excited, clutching their bundles. The boy with the message had run back to join them; she wasn't even sure now which one had spoken to her. She slipped away from them all and carried on down the track to the millrace. There was no one to be seen. Maybe whoever it was would be waiting behind one of the sheds. But if it was Lizzie, wouldn't she run out to meet her? What if it was Robin; sly, vengeful Robin? She paused. Her heart was pounding now, her feet dragging. I daren't look, I daren't, she thought. But then she heard her name urgently whispered.

"Em'ly! It's me!"

"Sam!" She ran behind the shed. Sam was standing with his arms folded, grinning as if he was a surprise birthday present.

"Sam! What are you doing here?" she gasped. "Where've you been? The wagon's coming soon. Don't miss it!"

"I don't want to go on that wagon, Em'ly. I'm never going back to that workhouse again."

"But what are you going to do?"

"I got somewhere to live! I had to see you before you go. I wanted to tell you, so's you don't think bad of me. That night of the fire, I didn't go to Oldcastle."

"I saw you running off to the woods. But I don't blame you, not now."

"I wasn't running away, Em'ly. I don't want you to fink that. I remembered, you see, cos I've been through those woods before on Sundays sometimes, I remembered you can cut right through them to the big road and there's a coaching inn on that road. I said to myself, if I get to it, someone there might send for the fire brigade quicker than going all the way down to Oldcastle."

"So that's how they came so fast! You saved the mill, Sam! It was really burning. And Master Crispin turned up too – I couldn't believe it when I saw him. I thought he was miles away."

"Would you believe it, he was at the inn! Cor, I nearly turned into a skelington when I heard his voice! His horse had gone lame, and he was fetching up for the night there before he carried on to New Mills. And I took courage and told him everything, all about Robin Small and the big lads and the fire, and he ran round the inn like a wild man and the people there all sent messages for helpers and the firemen and the police. Ooh, it was like a scurry of ants! I told Master Crispin I daren't go down Bleakdale because of Crick, and he said how about if I stayed and looked after his horse and I said I'll sleep in the stable with him. I love horses and me and my dad used to help out with them. And the innkeeper said 'e needed a horse-boy! It was my last chance, Em'ly, and I said yes, that could be me, sir! So he's kept me on. I live there now!" He hugged himself, his face round as a pumpkin with pleasure.

"Do you know what happened to Crick?" asked Emily.

"I don't. I'm that scared of meeting him again, I hardly sleep at night for jitters in case he finds me there in the stables."

"He died, Sam."

Sam stared at her, unbelieving. "Crick died?" He paused, then blew out his breath slowly, shaking his head. "Well, he nearly killed me a couple of times, but I wouldn't wish that on him. No, I wouldn't."

"They'll be wanting Robin for murder now, or manslaughter, won't they? They took the other boys away, the big ones that he went round with."

"They'd have took me too, if I'd been down there. But I'm not worried about them now. Master Crispin will vouch for me. I couldn't have set the mill on fire, and he knows that. Now you're all going back to the workhouse I can keep my job at the Coach and Horses inn and it's a dream come true. I didn't want to come near this place ever again in my life, but I wanted to see you, I wanted to tell you I didn't run off that night. I saw the masters talking to everyone just now and I hid round the back and listened. So now I know you're going today and I had to say goodbye to you. I must go, quick, what with the fright of Robin and the wagon coming and the innkeeper not knowing I've slipped down here, I must go. I must say goodbye, Em'ly."

Emily didn't know how to say goodbye to him. She held out her hand like a lady, and he put his arms round her and hugged her tight, his face still lit with smiles. Then he turned and slipped away, soundlessly, as if he'd never been there.

Emily stepped away from the shed. In one direction lay the apprentice house, where all the children were clustering together waiting for the wagon. In the other lay the mill. She could see Master Crispin now coming out of the gates of the house. He was wheeling his father down towards the mill. "Last chance, Emily," she told herself. "Be like Sam. You've got to take it. Any minute now you'll be hauled onto that wagon and you'll never know the truth." She went slowly up to where the two men were facing the ruin of their mill, and stood timidly near them. Master Crispin was talking excitedly, making plans, drawing ideas in the air, the older man grunting agreement. He seemed at last to sense that Emily was there, and motioned his son to wheel his chair round to face her.

"Master Blackthorn," Emily whispered. Her hands were clenched at her sides.

He stared at her, his dark eyes blazing with anger and sorrow. "I remember you," he said at last.

"Yes, sir."

"You're the girl who told me about the fire. Come for money, I suppose?"

"No, Master Blackthorn," Emily gasped. "I want to know about my sister."

The old man flapped his hands. "Your sister? Your sister? How on earth am I supposed to know anything about your sister?"

"Sir, she was hurt in one of your machines. She

was a scavenger. Miss Sarah took her into your house."

"That child again." Master Crispin interrupted. "You asked about her the other day, after church. And my mother told you she was dead, I believe. I heard her say that."

"I just wondered if she was mistaken." Away behind her Mrs Cleggins was calling the apprentice children together because she could hear the wagons coming for them. Soon, very soon, she would be called away, and she would never know the truth.

"Was that the sick child in Sarah's room?" Master Blackthorn frowned.

"Nonsense," Master Crispin said. "We'd have known about it if there was a child in the house."

"Oh, I knew about it all right. Nothing goes on in my house that I don't know about, Crispin. But I'd no idea it was a mill child. I thought she belonged to one of Sarah's friends. A scavenger, was she? In my house? Well – no, she didn't die."

"She didn't!" Emily sighed. "I knew! I knew!"

"Emily!" she heard Mrs Cleggins's voice, calling her. "Where's Emily Jarvis gone now?"

"Go on, you're being called for. Get away with

you," Master Crispin snapped.

Emily turned, and turned back again, desperate for more news. "But where is she? Please tell me."

"My daughter's taken her to the Wirral, to my wife's sister's. As far as I know, the child is well again."

Emily felt tears and sobs of joy rising now, swelling in her throat, bursting from her in a cry of relief and joy. She knelt down in front of the wheelchair and took both of his old mottled hands in her own.

"Oh, thank you! Thank you, Master Blackthorn! With all my heart, thank you!"

32

A Letter from Dr Barnardo

One afternoon, Sarah and Aunt Gillian were sitting in the library listening to Lizzie read. Lizzie's cheeks were flushed with excitement. The letters on the page were no longer spidery shapes and dots; they fitted together, they all made sense. Words made her laugh and cry, feel afraid, puzzled, angry, made her sigh with pleasure. They created thoughts and pictures in her mind, colours and feelings and voices. This story today was so exciting that she read rapidly and surely, letting her voice ring out with confidence. At the end of the chapter, she laid down the book and sighed, and then smiled up at her teacher.

"Wonderful, Lizzie!" Sarah clapped her hands. "You read every word perfectly – but what's more, you read with understanding; and you sounded as if you enjoyed it!"

"I did," Lizzie said. "I love this story! I want to read the whole book now!"

"And you will! And when you've finished that one, there's hundreds more here to read! You'll never forget how to read now, Lizzie. You half knew already, and now you've done it. You're a reader! You must read everything you see, and nothing will ever be a mystery to you."

"And that's enough for today! I think she deserves a nice drink, and a brisk walk along the beach," Aunt Gillian said. "Why don't you run down to the kitchen and ask Eglantine to make you a cup of cocoa, and then get your warm cloak. We'll all go for a walk!"

Lizzie put down the book reluctantly and went out of the room, passing Hetty as she came in with the day's letters.

"Three for me!" Aunt Gillian sighed. "Perhaps I won't get a walk, after all. I shall have to spend the whole afternoon answering these."

Lizzie paused in the doorway. She was curious to know what people said in letters. Now that she could write, she could send a letter to someone – anyone. *But I have no one to write to*, she thought. Again she stared into her past, and it was like peering into a dark tunnel. Sometimes she half heard a voice, someone speaking words that made no sense; she saw a girl with bubbly hair; heard a shriek of uncontrollable laughter. Sometimes there was an older girl with long hair the colour of straw. And then her image rippled like a reflection in water, and was gone; a fish flickering into the light and darting away to hide under stones.

She watched Aunt Gillian slitting open one of the envelopes with a paper knife and glancing rapidly down the page. "Ah – this is from Thomas Barnardo! You remember him, Sarah? That very earnest Irishman who went to Durham University with your cousin? He spent one of the vacations here with us. My goodness, he's asking for money! He must think I'm one of his wealthy associates. Setting up some kind of home for destitute children – oh dear, it's too sad. I can't read it now." She let the letter fall away onto the floor and began to slit open another. "No, I can't read this one either. This is from your mother, and I really can't be doing with her long missives just now. I'll save this for later too." She glanced up and saw Lizzie still standing there. "Hurry up, dear. Fetch your cloak!"

When Lizzie came back, the room was empty.

Aunt Gillian had obviously decided to walk with them after all, and had gone to fetch her own cloak. The opened letter lay on the floor where she had dropped it. Lizzie went over to it and picked it up, and idly let her eyes wander down the page. She couldn't read the scrawly handwriting, but there was a printed leaflet attached to the letter, easy to read. "Read everything you see, and nothing will ever be a mystery to you," Sarah had said. She began to scan the page, but two words in it caught her eye instantly. She read on, understanding nothing because the thoughts in her head were flittering like a flock of startled sparrows. Again she looked, and again, at the same two words. They opened themselves up, like birds unfolding their wings. She said them aloud, and she said them again. *Jim* was the first word. And the second word was *Jarvis*.

When Hetty came into the room a little later she found Lizzie clutching the leaflet in her hand.

"Oh, Lizzie," she chided her. "You mustn't go reading Miss Gillian's letters! Put it down quick, before she comes in."

Lizzie thrust the leaflet towards Hetty. "It says

my name! Look! Jarvis! That's my name. I remember now! My name is Lizzie Jarvis!"

Hetty shook her head, perplexed. "No good showing me, I can't read a word of it!" She could see that Lizzie was excited and perturbed, on the edge of tears. She put her arm round her, wanting to comfort her, but Lizzie was rigid. Her face was as white as death, and her eyes glittered. "I'll get Miss Sarah," Hetty said, and ran out of the room, flustered.

Miss Sarah came hurrying in and found Lizzie in the same state of excitement, scanning the leaflet and muttering the words on it to herself as if she could make no sense of them. But the colour had come back to her face now, hectic spots of red on her cheeks as if she was in a fever.

Sarah ran to her and tried to take the leaflet from her, "What's the matter, Lizzie? Are you ill again? Let me take this."

But Lizzie wouldn't let go. "It says Jarvis. It says Jim Jarvis," she kept saying, laughing and crying at the same time. "It's my name! Jarvis! And Jim, he's my brother. Jim Jarvis."

"Are you sure?" Sarah asked. Aunt Gillian came in behind her and Sarah motioned her not to speak;

Lizzie was in a trance, like a sleepwalker who mustn't be disturbed.

"There's Jim, and there's me, and there's – Emily," Lizzie said, staring ahead of her without focusing on anything. "That's it! Emily. And we lived at Mr Spink's house and he threw us out because Ma was too ill to pay the rent, and Ma took us to – to Rosie's! She left me and Emily there for Rosie to look after – and she and Jim went away – and Sam told us they were in the workhouse, and Ma died. She died!"

Now she came out of her deep trance and began to cry, and Sarah folded her in her arms as if she was putting wings round her, held her close, let her weep until there was no crying left.

"There, there!" said Aunt Gillian, deeply moved. "I'm terribly sad for you."

"But Lizzie, your memory has come back, and that means you are truly getting better. That's wonderful!" said Sarah at last.

"Where's Emily?" Lizzie asked, pulling herself away from Sarah. "Emily, my sister!"

Sarah frowned. "I don't know. Did she come to Bleakdale with you?"

"I think so. I think so." Lizzie was confused.

There were so many girls in her mind, so many faces. Was one of them Emily's? "I don't know."

"I think we should go for that walk now," Aunt Gillian suggested. "A good brisk walk will help you to think, it will clear your head of all those sorrows and mysteries. You can tell us anything you want."

Lizzie nodded. She clutched the leaflet in her hands as she walked between Sarah and Aunt Gillian along the shore, but she saw nothing of the sea that day, or the glinting sands or the wading birds. She saw faces from her past crowding round her as if they were jostling for attention. She kept saying things like "Sam said we'd have roast potatoes, but we didn't!" and "There was girl called the Lazy Cat, but the two Dearies didn't like her", and Sarah and Aunt Gillian smiled at each other over the top of her head. Lizzie felt as if she knew everything that had happened to her now, but there were still things she didn't understand. Why did she live here with Sarah and Aunt Gillian, dressed in yellow muslin instead of in the itchy blue smock of the apprentices, and why did she sleep in her own bedroom with a warm fire crackling in the grate and a silver mirror to see her face in, instead of in the cold, bare dormitory with the weeping, snoring apprentice girls?

As they approached the house they heard the sound of horses and carriage wheels dragging on the sandy drive.

"Visitors!" Aunt Gillian said. "That means extras for lunch, and Eglantine hasn't been warned. She won't be happy about that!"

From the shore they watched the coachman jump down and call out something. The stable boy ran from the back of the house. Hetty ran down the steps pushing a wheel chair, and Eglantine hobbled after her.

"Goodness me, it's my brother-in-law!" gasped Aunt Gillian. "He never leaves the mill at this time of year. Something must have happened."

"Father! Oh, he looks so frail!" Sarah said.

They both hurried forward as the old man was helped from the carriage and settled into his chair. Lizzie hung back, afraid and bewildered. She knew him at once. Had he come to drag her back to the mill, to force her to wriggle under the thundering machine again?

I won't go! I won't! she thought. *I'll run away rather than go back there.*

Mrs Blackthorn climbed down after her husband. "Oh, that dreadful dusty lane!" she complained. "I have sand all over me now!"

"What a lovely surprise!" Aunt Gillian said. "Both of you here at once!"

"Didn't you get my letter?" Mrs Blackthorn asked. She pulled a handkerchief out of her sleeve. "I felt sure you would have got it this morning. Don't you know about the fire? Ruined! We're ruined!"

And now there was someone else behind her, passing down bags and shawls. It was a girl. She climbed down slowly and gazed round her. She was dressed in apprentice clothes, and her long, yellow straw-gold hair hung loose and blowing across her face. She lifted her hand to sweep it back and she turned her head away from the house to look towards the sea. And now Lizzie knew for certain who it was.

"Emily!"

33

PLANS

It seemed to Lizzie that over the next few days she remembered everything that had ever happened to her in her life, except for the time between her accident and the moment she opened her eyes and saw Hetty sitting at her side. Now that Emily had come back to her she was looking and feeling better than she had ever done. The two sisters spent hours together walking along the beach, collecting shells, making patterns of pebbles and feathers. Lizzie taught Emily how to write her own name in the sand, and they laughed together when the tide nibbled the letters away. Sometimes they pushed Master Blackthorn in his chair to the bottom of the garden. He loved to just sit there, gazing out to sea.

One late afternoon Aunt Gillian asked if the whole family could eat out there at the bottom of the garden. Tables and chairs were carried out and set where they could watch the sunset. It was a beautiful evening, still warm, and the sea crimson with the light of the dying sun.

"I want you girls here too," she called, waving to Emily and Lizzie, who were turning away to go and eat in the kitchen with Hetty and Eglantine where they usually did.

"I never thought the day would come when I would share my table with a pair of scavengers," Mrs Blackthorn said, and although her voice was sharp with surprise, she said it with just a hint of the same dimpling smile as Aunt Gillian.

"We have things to discuss," Master Blackthorn said.

"I know. But I still feel Emily and Lizzie should be here," Aunt Gillian insisted. "Besides, I believe Emily cooked the pudding, so we may want to compliment her on it."

"As you wish." Mr Blackthorn flapped his hand to ask for his chair to be pushed to the table, and Lizzie ran to help.

The mill owner glanced round at them all: his wife, his daughter, his sister-in-law, Emily and Lizzie. They all watched him expectantly. No one could start eating until he said grace. "May the Lord bless our food, and may we always be thankful for it," he said, and he looked at the two children from below his quivering eyebrows. "Amen. Well, my first piece of news today, is that I have received a message from Crispin to say that Robin Small has been captured by the police and is in their custody, awaiting Her Majesty's pleasure."

Emily and Lizzie glanced at each other. *Robin Small, 'e leads us all.* Sam had nothing to be afraid of now, was Emily's first thought. He's safe.

"What will happen to him?" Lizzie asked.

Mrs Blackthorn glared at her. In her society, children were never allowed to speak at the table.

"I don't know, child," Master Blackthorn said slowly. "I know what the police will want to do with him. They'll want to hang him."

"Father, you must stop it," Sarah said. She jumped up from her chair and ran round to his. "Please, please do your utmost to save his life. He's a boy. He did evil things, terrible things, but you can't put it right by letting them take his life away. And some good has come of it all, you have to admit."

Her father raised his hand. "As usual, my dear

Sarah, you have a point. But I have other matters to think of first," he said. "I have to think about the future of Bleakdale Mill. I do have plans. It isn't mine any more. It's Crispin's, what's left of it. I have given it to him. The Blackthorn name is known around the world. I'm proud of it, and it's his to carry on, but not in the way it was. We were well insured, we have money to put things right; your mother is quite mistaken in saying that we are ruined. Far from it. Great changes are being made. It's exciting!" He mopped his brow with his napkin and turned to his wife. "So we must go back to Bleakdale for a while. I must see how Crispin is getting on there. I can't leave him to do everything on his own."

Emily lowered her head. She daren't look at him, or at anyone. Would he take her back with him? she wondered. And if he did, then what would happen? Where would she go?

"What can you do?" Aunt Gillian was asking him. "You aren't a well man."

"Not much, but I can think for Crispin, make decisions for him. There'll be a grand mill rising out of the ashes. We'll call it Phoenix Mill." He reached out for his wife's hand and pressed it to his lips.

"Phoenix Mill! I like the sound of that," she murmured.

"That's wonderful, Pa." Sarah smiled at Lizzie. "Do you know the story of the phoenix? It was a mythical bird that rose out of the ashes of a fire. I'll tell you all about it later."

But Emily and Lizzie weren't in the mood for mythical stories. If the mill was to be restored, must they go back to it? That was all they could think about. Would they become scavengers again, scrabbling on their hands and knees, bowing under the great weight of the monstrous machine that had nearly killed Lizzie? Lizzie pressed her hands to her ears, as if she could hear again the thunderous rumble above her head. They hardly listened to the rest of the conversation.

"Aye. Phoenix Mill," Master Blackthorn sighed. "And it will be known around the world – new equipment, modern machinery, fine textiles. I've minded what you said to me, Sarah. There'll be good conditions for the workers: safe machinery, meal rooms, cottages built in the valley. People will want to come and work at Phoenix Mill. They'll be proud to be employed by us." He raised his glass again.

"I'll drink to Phoenix Mill."

"But please tell me I don't have to go back there too," Sarah said. "There were things I loved about Bleakdale – the sound of the river, and the curlews crying over the moors in spring, and the shadows the clouds made on the hills. But I love here best."

"I'd like to ask you what your plans are then, Sarah?" He glanced over to Emily and Lizzie. "You girls had better buzz off. This is none of your concern."

Emily and Lizzie stood up to leave the table, anxious and silent, but Aunt Gillian raised her hand. "Stay here!" she said sternly, and they hovered, uncertain.

"I do have plans, yes, Pa," Sarah said. "I've been discussing them with Aunt Gillian, and I have her approval and her permission. I intend to stay here, but I don't intend to be idle. I have taken enormous pleasure in teaching Lizzie to read and write, and now I'm teaching Emily too." She smiled at them both. "And you two have taught me how to be a teacher! There are so many children around here who have never been to school – the children of farmers and fishermen, the cottage children. My plan is this"

– she hesitated, and took a steady breath – "to open a little free school for them in the barn at the bottom of the garden."

There was a moment's silence. "Teacher, eh?" her father said at last. "Well, you always had your nose stuck in a book, and this is what becomes of it. I dare say it's a good way of passing the time, till you get married."

"Pa!" Sarah said indignantly, and he reached across and pressed her hand. "Joking, my dear."

His wife harrumphed down her nose and set to eating Emily's pudding. "Excellent!" she announced. "I do like a good, sweet pudding."

"I have a plan too," Aunt Gillian said. "But first, the reason why I have asked the girls to stay at the table is so I can ask them what their plans are."

The tide was receding, and the gulls were following it out, keening their yearning, lost cry. Emily shook her head. *My plans?* Tears welled up in her eyes. How could she have plans, when her future was blank and unknown?

"I would like to go to a school like Miss Sarah's," Lizzie said shyly. "If ever I had the chance, that's what I would like to do."

"And Emily?"

"So would I," she nodded. "One day, I would."

Aunt Gillian smiled and exchanged glances with Sarah.

"And my plan is to make that happen for you. You have a home here, and I would like you to stay."

"Oh, Miss Gillian!" Emily blurted out.

"*Aunt* Gillian. If you wish to stay, that is."

"We do! We do!" shouted Lizzie. "Thank you! Thank you!"

"Thank you," repeated Emily, when her voice came back to her and she could speak.

34

ONE LAST THING

There was one more thing, before the dusk descended. The moon was rising, a few stars were flowering. The long, lost cry of the last curlew bubbled across the shore. Hetty brought out lanterns and set them on the table, and they all sat in silence, listening to the night, each thinking about their plans, their future.

Emily glanced round at them all while they were eating the pudding she had made. They were all together like a big family. What wonderful plans they all had. Master Blackthorn and his wife would return to Bleakdale to see the completion of Phoenix Mill, to make it better and bigger than it had ever been before. Sarah would open up her school here. She and Lizzie would read and learn every day, and one day they might even help Sarah in the school. She would help Eglantine in the kitchen and listen to her endless stream of chatter. And Aunt Gillian, funny, busy Aunt Gillian, would become their guardian.

She felt engulfed by it, by the kindness and the promises, by the sweet future that lay ahead like the sheen of the sun on the sea just outside the window. She daren't look at Lizzie. Life was nearly perfect. Nearly, after so much pain and darkness. Nearly.

Mrs Blackthorn said that it was time the pair of scavengers made their way to their room, and Emily and Lizzie slipped down from their chairs and shyly said goodnight. Sarah hugged them both.

Just before they left the table, Lizzie pulled a crumpled piece of paper out of her pocket and put it in front of Aunt Gillian, then ran after her sister. And there in the shadow of the house, they loitered, waiting and watching.

"Ah! Read this." Gillian pushed the paper towards her brother-in-law. Master Blackthorn grunted and fumbled for his spectacles.

"I can't read it in this light," he grumbled.

Gillian brought the lantern closer and read it out to him. "I have come across many children in London who are utterly penniless, totally destitute, with no parents, no money, no home. Shame on us all, if we can do nothing to help these children. I am determined to open a house for them to live in, where they will be given shelter, food, warmth, education, work and hope. This will not be a workhouse, but a family home. No destitute child will be refused admission. I am writing to ask if you would be prepared to send a donation towards this project, which is so very dear to my heart. I enclose a pamphlet describing the life of one of these street urchins, and I hope it will help you to understand how vital this cause is. Yours obediently, your humble servant, Thomas Barnardo."

"Barnardo, eh? I remember the chap," Master Blackthorn said.

"And this is the leaflet he sent with the letter. It's about a boy called Jim Jarvis."

She passed the leaflet to her mother, who read it slowly, and nodded. "This is such a worthy cause. It's too easy to forget about homeless children."

"There's more to it, Ma. Emily and Lizzie believe this boy might be their brother," said Sarah.

"Really! But if he is, he couldn't be in safer hands than Barnardo's," grunted Master Blackthorn. "A man of vision and passion. We will of course send a very large donation, as much as we can afford."

He glanced at his daughter, and there was a nod

of understanding between them. He reached across the table and took her hand in his own, and they both looked at Aunt Gillian.

"I have one more plan," Aunt Gillian said quietly. "Emily, Lizzie, come over here and join us. We have a lot of preparation to do. None of this can be hurried. This is my plan. One day soon, when Sarah's school is running, and you two girls are legally in my care " –she paused for a long, slow breath– "and when Thomas Barnardo's home for destitute children is opened, we will make a journey. Emily and Lizzie, you and I will go to London and we will pay a visit. I will take you to meet your brother."

Sarah smiled at the girls. "You'll have to be patient, but it will happen. You will see Jim again, I promise. What do you think?"

Emily put her arm round Lizzie. "It's perfect," she whispered.

"Yes," said Lizzie. "It is now. Everything is perfect."